DEVASTATE ME

A Next-door Neighbor Romance

EMMA CASTLE

Emma Castle Books

The publisher is not responsible for websites (or their content) that are not owned by the publisher.

ISBN: 978-1-952063-20-6 (e-book edition)
ISBN: 978-1-952063-21-3 (paperback edition)

For my father who served in Vietnam as an engineer in the Construction Battalion. I'm proud to be his daughter.

"Who is that?" Ophelia Wescott asked her new neighbor as they finished carrying in the last few boxes of Ophelia's belongings into the starter home she'd just purchased.

"Who?" the neighbor in question, Miranda Oakland, asked with a grunt as she set the box she'd been hauling down on the living room floor. Miranda was older than Ophelia, close to forty-five, as opposed to Ophelia, who was twenty-four, but Miranda was fun and energetic, and the age difference didn't even seem to exist between them. Ophelia had taken to her instantly when she'd introduced herself a few hours ago after the moving van had pulled into the driveway.

Ophelia approached the wide window in her

living room and pointed to the house on her left. "That. Who is *that*?"

There, mowing the lawn, was the most attractive man Ophelia had ever seen. He was at least six foot three, with dark hair the color of chocolate and a body that made a woman's thighs clench.

Miranda shadowed her at the window, and when she saw where Ophelia was pointing, she chuckled.

"Oh. That, my dear, is Colt Henshaw." Miranda sighed. "Isn't he gorgeous? Wait until you see those whiskey colored hazel eyes of his."

Ophelia leaned against the window as Colt stopped pushing the lawnmower and pulled his shirt up to wipe the sweat away from his face. The simple action showed the sharp vee of his abdominal muscles as they disappeared beneath his black basketball shorts. There wasn't an ounce of fat on Colt, as far as Ophelia could tell.

Miranda pretended to fan her face. "He has that effect on all of us. But don't expect him to notice you. It's not personal. He keeps to himself. Robert talked to him at one of the homeowners' meetings when he first moved here two years ago. He's a former Navy SEAL, I think."

"Really?"

"According to my husband, anyway."

Ophelia sighed. A Navy SEAL, just like the heroes in those romance novels she read. Of course, reality was nothing like those books. It was still fun to dream, though.

"Come on," Miranda said. "Let's get the rest of the boxes from your porch so you can send the movers home early."

"Thanks." Ophelia appreciated her new friend's help. She was new to Havensport and still a little tight on money. Sending the movers home early would save her a few bucks. Thankfully, she would be starting her new job tomorrow. Even though it would be a Sunday, she liked the work and didn't mind the unique schedule of working Sunday to Thursday.

"So, what's your job again?" Miranda asked as they each grabbed a box and headed back inside.

"I'm an online stylist. I select outfits, clothes, shoes, and accessories for clients based on their fashion profile, and then my company mails a box to them with the items I've chosen. They try the items on and buy what they like."

"Hmm, what will they think of next?" Miranda smiled at her, and then Ophelia quickly met the movers at the door as they carried in the last piece of furniture. While she was standing outside and writing a check for the movers, she caught a glimpse of Colt, who'd finished mowing and was now carrying an assortment of gardening tools. He halted at the invisible line between their two yards and knelt by a flower bed. Now she had a better chance to see his face. He had one of those masculine square jaws, outlined by a short beard. She'd never seen the appeal of a beard before, but on Colt? It was hot. A little *too* hot.

"You're as cute as a button, honey, but I promise you, that man isn't looking for anyone or anything. Best not to get your hopes up."

Ophelia sighed and turned away from the window. Miranda was right. Colt was a little too sexy, and she'd never had much luck with overly attractive guys anyway. She was only five foot two and a bit too much on the curvy side. Her last boyfriend had dumped her for a tall, leggy blonde. As a result, she'd decided to move—she wanted a fresh start in a new city. So she'd packed up her life and used her savings to buy this house. She wanted no regrets, and that included being shot down by her beyond hot, emotionally unavailable next-door neighbor.

COLT ALWAYS KNEW WHEN HE WAS BEING WATCHED. After serving fourteen years in the navy, he'd never lost that sixth sense of heightened awareness. He sat back on his knees by his front flower beds to pull weeds from the red azaleas in front of his house and shot a covert glance at the house to his right. The subtlety of this move would have made his former commanding officer proud.

The moving truck was pulling away, and his new neighbor was watching him through the large front window of her house. She had also watched him mow the lawn. He was used to the women in the neighborhood eyeing him anytime he was outdoors.

Last summer he'd been digging holes to plant tulip bulbs when two of the more aggressive divorcées in the neighborhood had actually parked folding chairs across the street, sipping margaritas as they ogled his ass like he was part of the *Magic Mike* crew in Vegas. He had allowed it, but he sure as hell hadn't liked it. He liked his privacy. He liked being left the hell alone.

Colt had a strange sense that his new neighbor was going to change everything. He had caught a glimpse of her, and she was a sweet young thing with big dark eyes and hair as black as a raven's wing. Her skin was a creamy pale like alabaster. He sure as hell didn't want to get interested in her. He was done with that sort of thing. He'd been burned, and he wasn't about to let this sweetheart next door get anywhere near him. She looked like she carried a pocketful of matches that just might set him ablaze.

He finished up his weeding and headed inside. His German shepherd, Noah, was watching him with dark, serious eyes from his favorite perch on the couch backed up against the window facing the street. At the sight of Colt, Noah's tongue lolled out, making him look like he was smiling. The dog had been trained to sniff out explosives, and after three tours of duty in Iraq, Noah had been allowed to retire. Colt had signed up to adopt the dog, and the two of them had stuck together. Given his rocky upbringing, Colt rarely spoke to his parents, and he had no siblings. Noah was the closest thing he had to family now.

Colt took a quick shower and changed into jeans and a T-shirt. Noah was waiting for him at the back door to the garage. "You want to go see the boys?" he asked as he retrieved Noah's leash.

The dog sat patiently, tail thumping as Colt leashed him up and then they got in his truck. He drove through the tiny main street of Havensport toward the VA center, where Noah worked on the weekends.

"Come on, boy." Colt led the shepherd into the center, and they were immediately surrounded by men and women, nearly all of them recovering from injuries, both physical and mental.

One man missing an arm from the elbow down had a big goofy grin on his face as he knelt to rub the dog's head. "Hey there, Noah. You're a good boy, aren't you?"

Colt gave the man a nod. "Hey, Charlie. How's the arm?"

"Wouldn't know. It's still somewhere in Afghanistan." Charlie laughed. "But seriously, the phantom pain is lessening now."

Colt looked at the other men and women who were crowded around the room. Each and every one had something they had sacrificed for their country. For some, the cost was physical. For others, it was mental. Colt had his share of scars like all the rest, but he'd suffered more emotionally in the end. While Colt didn't have night terrors or ever worry about hurting anyone near him, he had enough bad memories and nightmares to last him a lifetime. Yet at the same time, he knew he was luckier than the men and women here.

Colt unclipped Noah's leash and stood back, letting the therapy dog do his thing. Noah walked respectfully up to each veteran he encountered, sniffing their hands and letting the people pet him. There was a quiet nobility to the dog, as though he knew just how much his gentle, healing presence meant to the bruised and battered souls here. It made Colt proud to be Noah's owner. Not that he viewed Noah as property. They were a two-member unit. A family.

"Hey, Colt." Nancy, a former army sergeant, came over to him. These days, she helped run the VA center and took care of everyone like a mother hen. She offered a smile that made Colt relax. She was beautiful, with dark skin, rich brown eyes, and a head of tight black curls that reflected her natural excitement for life by the way they bounced on her shoulders.

"Hey, Nance, how's things?"

"Not bad." Nancy chuckled as Noah licked an older veteran's face enthusiastically. Then she turned back to Colt. "I heard from Dean."

Colt's entire body went rigid with fury.

"He was asking about you," Nancy continued carefully. "Wanting to know how often you came to the center."

"Wish I could say I give a fuck," Colt growled.

"Colt, I know what happened between you. I know it was bad, but you can choose to let it go, you know."

"When a man comes home from war, he doesn't expect to find his fiancée in bed with his best friend."

Colt wished more than anything that he could erase that memory. He'd come home from the naval base, exhausted, still recovering from a knife wound he'd gotten three weeks before. He'd dropped his bags on the floor and headed into the bedroom, only to find Talia with Dean, his best friend and fellow Navy SEAL. And they weren't talking over a cup of coffee while waiting for him.

His stomach still turned at the memory. He had taken one look at their faces, flushed with passion, and a part of him had died. He'd grabbed his bags, called a cab, and was halfway down the street before the cab found him. He hadn't even looked back. He'd returned to the naval base and made plans to move the next day.

"If Dean comes here looking for you . . . ," Nancy began.

"Tell him I'm dead." Colt was deadly serious. Whatever lay between him and his former friend was gone.

"Okay, tough guy, I get it," Nancy said with a wry smile. "So, what's new with you? Still afraid to go out and have fun?"

"I'm not afraid. I just don't want to." He said this a little too gruffly, which only made Nancy laugh.

She had never been afraid of him or what she called his "Heathcliff-like broody demeanor." He'd once asked her what she meant by that, and she'd handed him a book titled *Wuthering Heights*. He had never read much as a kid. Neither of his parents had been much for reading to him, or fostering a love of books.

After Nancy's teasing, though, he'd decided to read *Wuthering Heights*. He'd devoured that book, and it had actually spawned a love of reading. And Nancy had been right—he was the antihero Heathcliff, dark and brooding and holding on to an anger from a past wrong.

Anger was an emotion he understood. It was one he could control. It didn't drown him like despair or choke him like grief. It gave him fuel so he could face the day.

"Well, don't try to have *too* much fun, handsome. You'll break every girl's heart." Nancy stood up on tiptoe and brushed her lips over his cheek before she walked away.

Colt frowned as he put Noah's leash back on and took him home. He needed to hit the grocery store after he dropped Noah off, since he wanted some steaks to grill tonight. He just hoped he didn't run into any of those damned nosy housewives, or his new neighbor. There was only so much temptation a man could take, and the sweetheart next door had *irresistible* written all over her.

❧

OPHELIA STARED AT HER EMPTY FRIDGE. IT WAS plugged in and running, but it was completely bare, just like her cupboards. There was nothing left to do but go shopping. Normally she wouldn't mind that, but she was bone-weary from putting everything away and setting up her furniture the way she wanted. She grabbed her keys and purse and, with a resigned little sigh, left her new house. She really wished she had a few days to properly settle in before starting her new job, but at least she was working from home.

The grocery store in Havensport was small, but Miranda had assured her earlier that afternoon that it had everything she might need. As she parked and walked into the store, the sun was resting on the tops of the trees, painting the world in a beautiful golden glow. It was lovely here in this small coastal town. She might never have moved here if it hadn't been for an article on social media about how it was one of the quietest and loveliest places to live in Oregon.

Ophelia grabbed a shopping cart and started to peruse the aisles, trying to think of all the things she needed for the next week or so. She turned the corner and maneuvered around a huge tower of tuna cans that formed an endcap display, only to jerk to a halt at the sight of her new neighbor standing at the meat counter fifteen feet away.

Colt was leaning on the curved glass counter, talking to the butcher behind it. Ophelia ran her gaze over his hard, lean, and thoroughly developed body. His jeans hugged him just right, and his T-shirt clung to his broad shoulders and tapered waist like it had been painted on. He was sheer gorgeous masculine perfection with those high cheekbones and his square jaw. Her mouth ran dry at the sight of his forearms and the way his muscles flexed when he moved. His lips were fuller than she remembered, yet despite their innate sensuality, she knew they could purse into a foreboding scowl.

Colt accepted a package of meat from the butcher and set it into his basket before turning her way. In a panic, Ophelia swung her cart away, only to run into the endcap display of tuna. With a loud crash, the metal cans fell in an avalanche. Ophelia stumbled on the rolling discs and fell, her ankle twisting as she accidentally stepped on one of the cans.

"Ouch!" Her cart shot away from her as she cried out, heading straight toward a stand of locally harvested honey in glass jars. She closed her eyes, desperate not to see the inevitable disaster about to unfold.

But nothing happened. Colt had somehow bolted ahead and caught the front of her runaway cart, stopping it before it hit the jars. She opened her eyes and then saw him set his own small basket down and come over to her. His face darkened with a stony expression that made her light-headed. If he started yelling at her in the store, she'd make a run for it . . . assuming she could even walk right now. She tried to stand and winced as her ankle twinged. She could put her weight on it, but she wasn't running anywhere.

Colt's hand gripped her upper arm, holding her

steady. She stared up at his face as he pushed her cart back into her hands, giving her something to lean on.

"You okay, sweetheart?" His rumbling voice sent wild shivers of excitement through her. God, she'd never reacted to a man's voice like that before. And he'd called her *sweetheart*. Why was that so sexy? It shouldn't be, should it? Yet she wanted to melt into a puddle at his feet the second he called her that.

"I . . . Yeah, my ankle just got a little twisted." She tried to shake the sudden fog of desire that rose up around her. She was supposed to be focusing on being on her own, starting a new life and career, not dating. But that was hard to do when someone like this was standing so close. The man was a solid wall of masculinity that made her tremble.

"Your ankle?" His hazel eyes swept down her legs with hawklike precision. She flushed as she realized she must look like crap right now, dressed in a pair of old shorts and a T-shirt. Her hair was even pulled up in a messy bun. This was *not* how she had pictured having her first—or any—face-to-face meeting with Colt. It wasn't fair that men could shower and throw on clothes and look fine, but women needed to schedule in advance.

Colt's dark brows lowered with obvious frustration at her lack of response. "Can you walk?"

"Yes. I can." She would walk out of there even if it

killed her. *Stupid tuna cans* . . . She wasn't a klutz, but he would probably assume she was now.

"Good. You sure know how to make an entrance, sweetheart." He extended his hand and said, "I'm your new neighbor, Colt Henshaw."

Ophelia placed her hand in his and his warm hand closed around hers in a surprisingly gentle squeeze despite his strength.

Colt looked at the cans of tuna still rolling around. A young man wearing a grocery store apron was trying to collect the cans still cruising down the aisles.

"They'll never let me come back here," she moaned. There had to be at least a hundred cans of tuna to pick up. "Sorry! So sorry!" she called out to the clerk, whose face was flushed as he tried to gather up the cans.

"It will be fine. He's probably glad your cart didn't hit the honey. He'd be mopping that up for hours."

"Oh God, don't remind me. If you hadn't caught the cart . . . Thank you for that, by the way."

"You're welcome." After they helped the clerk pick up the cans, he nodded at her purse. "Give me your list. I'll get what you need, and you can wait up front for me. Rest your ankle."

Was he serious? It was hot that he wanted to do something like that for her, but also a little insulting that he just ordered her what to do. She had the strange urge to defy him, then maybe kiss him, hard. Ophelia wasn't used to battling such a dichotomy of emotions when it came to men.

"I didn't bring a list. I was so tired from unpacking that I just drove straight over."

"Ah," he murmured in understanding.

"And thank you, but I really am okay. I can shop for myself."

The dubious look he gave her would have pissed her off if she hadn't been so damn tired.

"Wait here." His tone brooked no argument. He walked back to the meat counter and spoke to the butcher, who handed him another package of meat. Then he came back to her.

"We'll get you the essentials." Colt set his basket inside her cart and then took control of the cart. He was definitely former military, someone who just took charge.

"Seriously, you don't need to—" But he was already pushing her cart down the next aisle.

"You have no food, and you're tired. I was planning to cook steak tonight, and I don't mind tossing an extra one on the grill for you." He stopped next to the baking supplies, grabbing several items for her. "You aren't one of those girls who doesn't eat meat, are you?"

"No, steak is fine, but—"

"Then come to my place tonight at seven."

"Oh, what the hell. Thank you." She sighed and kept pace with him as he continued to fill her cart. "Fabric softener?" She was surprised that he put that in the basket. Her last boyfriend hadn't even known how to turn on the washing machine.

"What? Surprised that I'm a civilized man?"

She swore she detected a hint of humor in his tone and couldn't resist teasing him back. "No, I'm sure you're quite civilized. Anyone who has azaleas growing like you do has to be."

Despite his beard concealing his expressions, she caught a small smile. He didn't speak much as they filled up the rest of her cart. Normally, Ophelia would have been tempted to try to coax more answers out of him, but she was too tired.

"I'm Ophelia Wescott, by the way. I wasn't sure if you knew or not. Miranda said the homeowners' association emailed a newsletter this morning, but I wasn't sure who read it."

He snorted. "I never read that crap, unless I need to fall asleep."

"You don't? I *never* would've guessed you're the type to buck convention, Mr. Broody McBroodster." She didn't mean to reply so sarcastically, but she tended to get cranky when she was tired.

It didn't seem to faze him. "Mr. Broody McBroodster?" He chuckled, the sound almost warm and welcoming. But he glanced at her as they reached the self-checkout.

"You scan, I'll bag."

"Sir, yes sir." She gave a mock salute, expecting him to get prickly, yet he smiled again, and damn if that didn't send all sorts of wonderful butterflies tumbling around her stomach.

"So, Ophelia . . ." He spoke her name as they started scanning and bagging.

"Yeah, I know, it's a mouthful. That's what happens when your mother's an English professor."

But to her surprise, he closed his eyes and began to recite something from memory:

Do not, as some ungracious pastors do,
*   Show me the steep and thorny way to heaven,*
*   Whiles, like a puffed and reckless libertine,*
*   Himself the primrose path of dalliance treads,*
*   And recks not his own rede.*

Ophelia stared at him. The man had just quoted from *Hamlet*, a passage spoken by the character Ophelia. She wasn't a huge Shakespeare fan, but her mother was, and she'd spent countless nights listening to her mother read it aloud when she was a child.

"You've read *Hamlet*?" As if she needed another reason to like him, the man could quote literature.

"You seem surprised."

"Not surprised in a bad way. I thought only my mother could quote Shakespeare off the cuff like that. Color me impressed."

"I'll admit I didn't actually enjoy Shakespeare as much as other things I've read. But I wanted to challenge myself. I've even read Chaucer and learned about the Great Vowel Shift around the time Middle English was in use. Not easy shit to learn."

"Chaucer? Wow, you really *do* like a challenge!" Ophelia chuckled.

His hazel eyes met hers. For a second, she was lost in his gaze, her heart fluttering, until he broke the spell by looking away once the last bag was filled. They quickly paid for their groceries, and he walked her to her car.

"Remember, seven tonight. Noah and I will be waiting." And with a devastating, panty-melting smile, he walked away across the parking lot.

Ophelia stared after him, wondering what she'd gotten herself into, and she was more than a little worried about who Noah was.

2

Ophelia crept across her lawn in the growing dusk, wearing a brightly colored blouse, jean shorts, and sandals. She hoped that none of her new neighbors would see her heading toward Colt's house. The last thing she needed was to be the center of neighborhood gossip. With a furtive glance around, she knocked on the navy-blue front door. The door opened, and Colt stood there, towering over her. She stepped back, far too aware of how close they were.

His strong body emanated heat, and she could smell a blend of fabric softener and lemon. Had he been doing laundry and cleaning . . . just for her? She wanted to think so. There was something sexy about a man who rushed to clean up his place for a woman coming over. It made her think of tumbling onto clean sheets with him and having insanely hot sex on them.

God, when had she become turned on by things like *that*?

"Come on in. I just fired up the grill." He stepped back, and Ophelia entered his home, her eyes darting around the room to note the cozy yet masculine furniture choices. It wasn't spartan by any means, but the color tones of the walls and furniture were in natural and neutral tones of dark browns, dove grays, and warm leather.

"So, am I the first to arrive?" she asked.

"What do you mean?"

"Your friend, Noah, wasn't it? Is he here yet?" For a second, Colt simply stared at her, inscrutable as ever, and then he laughed. The rich, deep sound made her think of him in bed. If she was honest, everything he did was making her think of him in bed.

"Noah!" He whistled sharply, and Ophelia tensed at the sound of nails scraping on wood floors. An impressive but intimidating German shepherd rushed into the room. Ophelia immediately shrank back, and that didn't escape Colt's notice.

"Afraid of dogs?" he asked. He waved a hand, and Noah sat where he was and then lay down.

"No, not exactly. I got bit by a German shepherd when I was twelve. The neighbor boys sent it after me as a joke. I still have a scar." She pointed to her chin.

Colt reached up and caught hold of her chin, leaning in to examine it. She knew he saw the tiny faint white scar at the bottom of her chin.

"Feeling brave?" he asked, and for some reason that made her heart race.

"Maybe?" She felt unsure, despite the fact that she had wanted to sound confident. Colt took her by the hand and led her to the large dog, who remained in his lying down position.

"Noah, this is Ophelia." He looked to her as he introduced them. "Noah is a therapy dog. He was a bomb sniffer in Iraq for three years. You won't meet a gentler dog, I promise." Colt knelt on one knee and motioned for her to do the same. Ophelia did, but she reflexively gripped Colt's arm. His skin was warm and comforting.

"You can pet him. He won't move from this position until I tell him to."

Trusting Colt, she reached out and patted the German shepherd. His fur was smooth and soft. The dog licked his lips, which made her flinch.

"That means he likes it, not that he sees you as a T-bone steak," Colt explained. "When dogs are feeling safe and content, they lick their lips like that." Sure enough, Noah's eyes half closed as though he was experiencing pleasure.

"How do you know so much about dogs?" she asked.

Colt smiled a little. "Always had them growing up. When I came home from my last tour, I signed up to adopt a retired military working dog. Noah has been through hell, and he's a damn good dog."

Ophelia assumed that Colt must have been through hell during his service as well. "Miranda mentioned you were a Navy SEAL?"

"Yeah." It was all he said, but it was enough. She knew what hardships servicemen and women faced.

She was still holding his arm when she spoke softly to him. "My dad was in the navy. He was a SeaBee, an engineer. I thank you for your service."

Her words caught him by surprise. She could see it in his eyes as he looked down at her. He didn't say anything for a long moment.

"I need to get the steaks on the grill." With a wave of his hand, Noah followed him out into the backyard. Ophelia joined him, and he nodded toward an outdoor table and chairs.

"Have a seat." He turned his back to her, lifted the grill lid and started laying the steaks across its surface. Noah settled down on the grass, and Ophelia sighed and relaxed a bit around him. He really was a beautiful dog.

The evening sunlight sank beneath the trees, and

some string lights hanging on the back porch suddenly came on, making her feel warm and cozy as the chilly air crept in around them. Ophelia was content to lean back in her chair and watch Colt cook. He mastered the grill, and in no time he presented her with a steak and a tin-foil-wrapped baked potato on a plate.

"You want a beer or something?" he asked.

"Sure, I'll take a beer."

He stepped into the house and returned with a dog bowl in one hand and two beers in the other. He handed her one bottle of beer and set his down before he cut up a third steak and mixed it into Noah's bowl of dried food.

Ophelia bit her lip to hide a smile. "You feed him steak?" It was clear he loved his dog.

"Only on Saturdays. Chicken and beef have all the nutrients dogs need that they don't get in dog food. It keeps them a little healthier and happier." Colt set the bowl down on the ground, and Noah dug in enthusiastically.

Ophelia had a thousand questions she wanted to ask, but she had never met anyone like Colt before, someone whose every look and action screamed that he was closed for business.

"So, Colt, what do you do now? Aside from being a good gardener." She kept her tone teasing, hoping to coax him to open up a bit.

"Private security. Consulting. Mostly online these days."

She expected him to ask her the same question, but he didn't. He took a long sip of his beer instead, his hazel eyes too hawklike as they studied her while she tried her dinner. It was perfectly cooked and tasted amazing.

"You want to tell me why you moved here?" he asked.

She stared at him. "What do you mean?"

"This is an out-of-the-way place. Young kids like you don't come here, not without a reason."

"I'm not young," she protested. "How old are you?"

"Old enough, sweetheart. I've lived a decade longer than you. I retired from the navy two years ago at age thirty-two. Feels like a lifetime."

So he was thirty-four? That wasn't old.

"How do you know my age?" she asked. "Or was that a guess?"

"No guess. I like to know who I live next to. I do a background check on everyone who moves to this neighborhood."

"Well, that doesn't sound suspicious or paranoid at all."

"It's not what you think. I work in security, remember? I'm sort of the neighborhood watch in these parts. We don't get a lot of crime, but there have been some nasty break-ins, and the police haven't caught whoever's been doing it. A couple of the homeowners were home, and one ended up in the hospital. So I try to keep tabs on those who are most vulnerable, to help make sure they stay safe."

"Oh, that makes sense."

"So, why Havensport?" he asked.

"I just wanted to get away," she replied. "There's nothing wrong with that." She ate another piece of steak.

"Well . . . Whatever reason you ran away, don't let life force you to hide."

"I'm not running," she protested.

Colt acted like he didn't hear her. "And for God's sake, don't make friends with the housewives in the neighborhood. Miranda and her husband are nice, but the rest . . ." He scowled as he trailed off.

"I heard you have quite the fan club."

"Fan club." He grimaced. "They need a goddamn hobby or better yet, jobs."

Ophelia smirked. "I think you're it."

"I wish they would just leave me the hell alone."

"Sorry. You're too handsome for that, so you might as well get used to it. Or maybe work it to your advantage."

Colt's brow furrowed. He obviously was not following her.

"You know, offer gardening services? Strip club rules, look but don't touch? You could make a mint."

She couldn't resist teasing him. She wanted to see him smile.

"Or maybe I'll mow my damn yard naked and charge admission for the show." He grinned darkly, as though the idea brought him a little too much joy.

Ophelia shook her head. "The logistics wouldn't work. Too many people could watch from their windows for free. Maybe if you did it as a fundraiser. If they raise X amount of money, you do the yard work naked."

"I'm sure the HOA would have something to say about that."

"Yeah, but who do you think is *on* the HOA?" she said, chuckling. "But yeah, you're probably right. Besides, you might cause a car wreck, and I'm sure that would end up in the HOA newsletter."

He almost smiled again. "You have a point."

After a moment, he collected the plates and headed inside. Ophelia stayed on the back patio, admiring the beds of flowers and the hardy maple trees that sheltered his decent-sized yard.

A squirrel scampered down one of the trees. In a burst of speed, Noah chased it right back up the trunk. Ophelia giggled and tucked her feet up in the large chair, feeling content for the first time in a long while. Right now there was nowhere she'd rather be.

Her bruised heart felt healed in some small way, for the first time since her breakup. And she had a bearded Navy SEAL who didn't like people to thank for it. What a strange thing life was.

❧

Colt put the dishes into the dishwasher and watched Ophelia laugh as Noah chased some squirrels. His chest tightened unexpectedly. How many nights had he and Talia spent like this? A few, most of them nice, but he'd been too young, too foolish to sense her unhappiness. A quiet life in a small town had never been her plan. She had wanted him to stay in the service and to work his way up the ranks so she could be a high-powered military wife and travel the world with him. There was nothing wrong with that, but she had never really understood what it meant to be in the service, nor what it meant to be married to someone who was.

A spouse of a service member gave up a lot, starting with a normal life. He'd met many men and women who took their roles seriously, and their dedication to helping the others on military bases mattered a hell of a lot. But Talia had only wanted the fun and none of the sacrifices. Colt had not been the man destined to make her happy.

When he had talked to Ophelia about running

away to a place like this, he'd wanted to warn her not to be like him. Yet as he watched her now, a peaceful smile on her face, he realized maybe he was wrong. Maybe she needed the sleepy town as much as he did.

Ophelia finally rose from her chair and came inside. "Can I help you put anything away?" She looked bone-tired, as she had in the grocery store.

"No, it's all taken care of. You should get home and sleep."

"Oh . . . okay." He didn't miss the note of disappointment in her voice and had to fight the urge to keep his distance. He followed her to the front door, where she turned to face him.

"Thank you for tonight. I hope you'll think of me as a friend. I could sure use one in a new town."

She looked so damn sweet, so vulnerable in that moment that all of Colt's instincts just flew out the window. She turned, a hand resting on his doorknob, but he caught her other arm, gently spinning her around and pulling her toward him. She was so small and curvy. She fit right against him as he cupped the back of her head. His hand buried itself in her dark hair, which tumbled in loose waves down her shoulders. It felt like silk, and he groaned inside as it slid against his skin, tickling him.

She stared up at him with those doe-brown eyes of hers, framed by thick sooty lashes, her pale-pink lips parted. He knew he was a goner.

He lowered his head to hers, his blood pounding in his ears. Her lashes fluttered closed, and she melted in his arms in the most wonderful way. They were drawn together like a pair of stars circling each other as gravity pulled them in for a cosmic explosion.

Colt's mouth covered hers in a gentle, searching kiss that Ophelia answered. Her hands clutched his shoulders and then slid up around his neck. A new urgency drove him as she opened her lips to his and he slipped his tongue inside, deepening the kiss. She tasted sweet, and she kissed so perfectly, a tender eagerness in her that made him feel like a teenager in the back of his dad's old Buick, trying to get to first base.

She tasted innocent, but she wasn't inexperienced. She met him kiss for kiss, leaving his body on fire with a growing hunger for more. He answered her with a savage intensity, drinking in as much of her as he could, his hands roaming over her, exploring her, the flare of her hips, the curve of her spine, and the feel of her shoulders and face as he touched her wherever he could.

A dreamy intimacy cloaked him as he made love to her mouth, showing her what he desperately wanted to do to her body. He wanted to spend hours with her in bed on Sunday mornings, kissing every inch of her after he'd given her such sweet pleasure that she would never want to leave.

He clutched her to him a moment longer before he heard Noah bark. Their mouths parted, the spell broken. He still held her hips, their bodies touching as they gazed at each other in shocked silence. Her lips were swollen and wet, and her eyes glowed with desire, but he could see she was coming back to her senses, like he was.

For a second neither of them moved or spoke. Then she blushed.

"Uh-oh . . ."

Uh-oh didn't even begin to cover the trouble they were both in.

3

Last night had been a big mistake. She shouldn't have let him kiss her. This move was supposed to give her time to breathe, to forget about guys and relationships and just let her focus on herself for a bit. Yet Ophelia kept replaying that kiss over and over in her mind. She had just asked him to be friends, and he'd pulled her into his arms and given her the most amazing kiss of her entire life. She hadn't known a kiss could feel like that, like the beginning and end of the world all at the same time. Yet it had, and she couldn't look at his house anymore without thinking about that kiss.

She forced her eyes away from the window and settled at her desk in the small room just off the dining room to begin her work. She logged in and spent the next few hours reviewing customer fashion profiles and matching their needs to a variety of potential items that could be packed and shipped off, along with a personal message to each customer. When it was five o'clock, she logged off and headed to the kitchen to figure out what to do with the rest of her Sunday.

The doorbell rang. Miranda was there at the door waiting, along with two other women.

"Miranda!"

"Hey, Ophelia. I brought two of the gals I mentioned yesterday. This is Eliza and Jennifer."

Ophelia remembered. According to Miranda, they were two of the more interesting divorcées on the street. They seemed nice, but Ophelia sensed they would love to know every little detail that Ophelia could share about Colt, now that she was living next to him. But she wouldn't talk about him, if she could help it. She was determined to have Colt as her friend, and would not betray his confidence. The last thing she would do was tell these women about how earth-shattering his kisses were.

"You off work, honey?" Miranda asked.

"I just finished for the day. What's up?"

"We ladies have an unofficial Sunday-night drink club. We would love for you to join us."

Drinks did sound nice right about now.

"I'd like that." She followed the ladies across the street to Jennifer's home. There was a long porch in the front of the house with cozy hanging benches and brightly covered deck chairs facing the street. Ophelia chose a chair and accepted a glass of white wine from Eliza.

"So, you settling in okay?" Miranda asked once everyone had drinks and was comfortably seated.

"Yes, I unpacked most of my stuff yesterday."

Eliza leaned forward, smiling deviously. "Okay, let's get to the good stuff, girls. Ophelia, we know you went over to Colt's last night. Dish, girl. It's a part of our Sunday-night ladies' code."

"How did you—?"

"I saw you," Jennifer said. "My kitchen window faces the street."

Oh boy . . .

"It's not what you think. I ran into Colt at the store, and he helped me after I tripped and fell."

Eliza nodded. "The tuna incident? Yeah, we heard."

"You heard?" Ophelia didn't know whether she should laugh or shake her head.

Jennifer waved a hand. "Small town. Word travels, honey. Continue."

"Anyway, I was exhausted, and he offered to cook me dinner since he was already grilling."

"Wait, he offered to cook dinner? Or was he like, 'I'll just throw a steak on the grill'?" Miranda asked.

"Definitely the latter."

Eliza sighed in disappointment. "Shame. I thought for sure we'd found someone he would like."

"What?" Ophelia prayed to God these women weren't trying to play matchmaker with Colt . . . or her.

"He's our brooding resident bachelor. It's fun to see if we can catch his attention with someone," Jennifer explained. "When he first moved in, I mowed my lawn in my bikini for two months just to see what he would do. I had the best tan that year, but he never gave me the time of day."

Ophelia was surprised by that. Even entering their forties, both Eliza and Jennifer were gorgeous women in their own right, and they were way more confident about themselves than she was. If Colt hadn't looked at them twice, she didn't stand a chance.

Then what about that kiss?

That might have just been a one-time thing. Maybe it was the alcohol. Maybe it was just an opportunity he took but instantly regretted. The thoughts made her heart sink.

"We thought he might be looking for someone, you know, a little younger. Ever since Miranda described you, we've all been dying to see what Colt will do."

As if on cue, Colt's front door opened and he stepped outside, Noah on his heels, leashed and clearly excited.

"It's five thirty, girls. Here we go." Miranda leaned back in her place on the swinging bench and sipped her wine.

"What happens at five thirty?" Ophelia asked in a whisper.

"Colt goes running with his dog. Every night at this time."

They all turned to watch him head in their direction as he walked down the sidewalk toward the street. He wore basketball shorts and a tank top that showed off his perfectly toned arms. He didn't even glance their way as he started to jog, his dog keeping pace.

"It's got to be the military lifestyle. He rarely misses a run." Miranda kicked her legs against the porch floor to make her bench swing a little.

"So back to this dinner," Eliza prompted. "What's his house like inside?"

"Normal?" Ophelia wasn't sure what these women expected. "A bit masculine, for sure, but it's cozy and nice. His backyard is lovely. He really has a talent for gardening."

"No kinky sex dungeon?" Jennifer asked. Eliza smacked her arm.

"What? No. I mean, I don't know. I only saw the living room, kitchen, and backyard."

"Ah, thank goodness, that leaves the basement. I

was having the best fantasies of him in one of those sex rooms with toys and stuff. *Fifty Shades* style."

Eliza snorted. "You would. If he and I were together, we wouldn't *need* toys."

Ophelia watched Eliza and Jennifer trade barbs. Miranda rolled her eyes with an indulgent smile and continued to drink her wine.

The conversation soon turned to other topics—children, ex-husbands, the latest local scandals of who was building some god-awful shed or who was not keeping their lawns up to code. Ophelia sipped her wine and gazed at Colt's house, unable to avoid thinking about him and his bedroom and his imaginary sex dungeon and all the things that might happen there. She shouldn't fantasize about him, she really shouldn't, but it was hard not to with the images the ladies had put into her head.

Ophelia didn't know what he would be like in bed, not from that one kiss, but she could imagine. The kiss had started soft and insistent, but he'd deepened it and his hands . . . they had been everywhere. Possessive, cupping and stroking in an almost dominant way but not quite. Would he be the kind of man who wanted to tie her up and fuck her hard? Or would he be slow and sweet, taking his time to draw out an endless orgasm? The only thing she was sure of after that one kiss was that he would devastate her.

After her breakup with Jack, she wasn't sure she

wanted a man to have that kind of power over her again. And she hadn't even been wildly in love with Jack. They had enjoyed being together, but it was more like companionship than love. And yet being dumped by him had hurt so much. The idea of liking a man even more than that? Of loving someone and getting her heart broken? That was the last thing she needed. Colt would have to devastate her only in her deepest, darkest fantasies.

※

COLT WAS DETERMINED TO BE ON HIS BEST behavior. He had made it a full two months now without kissing Ophelia since she had moved in. Everything felt almost normal.

Almost.

He'd gotten into the habit of taking walks in the morning with Noah, and one morning Ophelia had just sort of joined him. Now they'd been meeting up to walk every day since. Then it had seemed only natural that he'd come over to her house a few times a week to help weed her front flower beds. He'd also carried bags of mulch for her, since she was so damn small.

They'd had drinks at her place more than once, and he'd found himself talking about his past, his parents, the rough times he'd had as a teen, and how he'd ended up in the navy.

In turn, she'd told him all about her life back in Portland and how she'd gotten burned out working for a fancy fashion designer who'd yelled at everyone all the time. Colt had never laughed so hard as when she told stories about the fashion industry and all the crazy personalities involved.

They really had become friends, just as Ophelia had told him she'd wanted. Colt, to his own surprise, didn't mind that at all. In fact, it gave him an incentive to get up in the mornings. Noah was crazy about Ophelia and had apparently decided that his training to stay in place or heel did not apply whenever Ophelia was in sight. Colt wasn't mad—he could understand the dog's desire to bound up to her and lick her. Hell, he had the same desire to run up and grab her and kiss her senseless. He had done nothing since the night of the kiss two months ago but fantasize about Ophelia naked and making love to her until she cried out in exhausted pleasure.

The fantasies didn't stop there. He was not a man who was shy in bed. He could be rough and playful, sweet or dirty depending on his mood, and he kept running through every delicious scenario he could imagine of how he would taste Ophelia. Colt had never jacked off in the shower so much in his life as he had since she had moved in. He'd become as horny as some teen, getting hard at the sight of her just walking to her mailbox, or while she watered her potted plants in her backyard and he could hear her humming. The woman was a damn temptation, and if he didn't keep his shit together, he would give in to his need.

In order to stay out of trouble, he'd been visiting the VA center almost every other day after work, and it was where he was headed now, to keep his thoughts decidedly away from the tempting girl next door.

"I think you're coming here too often," Nancy teased as he and Noah walked into the center.

"You can't ever spend too much time with your fellow veterans," he replied, and he meant it. The veterans in their country were always forgotten. They'd served and sacrificed and went silent while others whined about shit they wouldn't even have if not for people like them who'd kept them safe. The irony was how that same tough silence meant they were increasingly overlooked—by the public and far too often by the government. The thought always made Colt furious.

"Hey, turn that frown upside down," Nancy teased. "Tell me what's going on. You've been amped up for the last couple of months."

Colt leaned against the wall of the lobby, which had filled with veterans who came to visit Noah. "Just neighborhood shit," he grumbled.

"Are those divorcées mowing their lawns in bikinis again? You poor baby." Nancy's playful sarcasm didn't go unnoticed. "Have you ever thought about dating again? You would put off those nosy neighbors, and you might actually have a good time yourself. You weren't born to be a monk, Colt. God gave you that body so women could enjoy it."

He definitely wasn't born to be a monk, but the woman he wanted didn't deserve a casual hookup. Ophelia was the kind of girl a man married and worshiped the rest of his life, and Colt wasn't sure he was ready for that after Talia.

"Nance, what Dean and Talia did—"

"It sucks, I know. But not every woman is like her. Most of us are pretty damn loyal and awesome." She gave him a pointed look, and he curled an arm around her shoulders.

"You are awesome, Nance. Why don't I just date you?"

She laughed heartily and nudged him in the ribs with an elbow. "I'm flattered, but you aren't my type, honey. I like 'em with blond hair and blue eyes." Her gaze betrayed her as she watched a tall blond-haired man roughing up Noah's fur, much to the dog's enjoyment. The man had one leg amputated below the knee, and he was wearing a prosthetic limb.

"Don't tell me you're shy?" Colt teased.

"Maybe a little, at least with that hottie," Nancy admitted.

"Hey, bro!" Colt called out. Nancy gasped and tried to run away, but Colt held her in place. "Nancy here wants to go out with you."

The man took one look at Nancy and came right over.

"I'm going to kill you, Colt," Nancy warned before turning on her bright smile as the soldier joined them. Colt took the opportunity to retrieve Noah, and then they headed to the parking lot. He was just putting Noah in the truck when someone called his name. He closed his truck door and turned, expecting to see someone from the center.

Colt's hands clenched at his sides as he recognized the man. Dean Griffin walked toward him, his hands held up, obviously hoping to avoid a fight.

"Hey, man, I've been trying to call you for months."

"I blocked your number." The last thing he wanted was to talk to the man who had ruined his life.

"Just give me a minute, okay?" Dean begged.

Colt looked down and saw the glint of silver on Dean's ring finger. "You married her, didn't you?" God, this day was going to shit fast.

"Yeah, I did, but—"

Colt threw three punches before Dean could finish. The blows sent Dean sprawling on his ass.

"Fuck!" Dean gripped his face with one hand, spitting blood. "You and your fucking haymakers, Colt, Christ. I forgot how much I hated fighting with you." He climbed to his feet and stood there, his guard lowered. "Go ahead. Hit me, man. I owe you that."

For a second, Colt's pulse spiked as his blood roared in his ears, but Noah's barking interrupted his building adrenaline. He calmed. Dean wasn't the enemy. He was a cheating asshole, nothing more.

"I'm sorry, Colt. I fucked it all up. I betrayed you. I betrayed our friendship. I know what we had is gone, but I had to find you and tell you I'm sorry. That's all." Dean was quiet, honest, and for the first time Colt felt the hot anger inside him begin to fade.

"I heard you'd been looking for me. How did you find me?"

"Vets talk." Dean chuckled. "You weren't that hard to find. I drove two hours to get here, but it was worth it." He held his jaw. "Well, except for that part."

Colt sighed. "So, you and Talia?"

"Married six months ago." Dean smiled wryly. "She's pushing me to go after promotions."

"You always were more ambitious than me."

"I suppose," Dean agreed. "Anyway, I'm sorry I surprised you."

"It's fine . . . now." If he had seen Dean two months ago, Colt would have thrown more than one punch. But things had changed. *He* had changed. Somehow that one kiss with Ophelia had set something in motion. He wasn't quick to change, but he was like molten lava beneath the surface, rolling, tumbling, burning, and perpetually changing inside.

"I wish things had turned out different," said Dean.

"Yeah, but they didn't. And maybe it's for the best."

Dean held out a hand to Colt, who stared at it for a long second. He thought of Ophelia and what she would want him to do, and then he placed his palm in Dean's, giving it a shake before letting go.

"Well, I should go." Dean nodded at him and turned to walk away.

"Take care, Dean."

"You too, man."

Colt gave himself a moment before he got into his truck and drove home.

It was early evening when he pulled into his driveway. Ophelia was out in her front yard, spreading mulch in the beds planted against her house. The sight of her cute butt in the air as she bent over made him smile, and he got hard thinking of all the sweet, wicked things he could to if she was bent over in front of him.

Maybe Nancy was right. Maybe he was brave enough to trust his heart to someone again. Maybe it was time.

She waved when she saw him. "Hey, Colt!" She came over, and her vibrant smile began to fade. "What happened to your hand?" She removed her gardening gloves and tossed them to the ground.

"What?" He looked down and saw the knuckles of his right hand were bruised and bloody.

"Let me see." She took his hand and pulled it toward her. "You have a first aid kit?"

He nodded toward his place. "In the house."

"Let's get you cleaned up." She grasped his wrist so as not to hurt him. God, she was sweet. He was perfectly capable of tending to himself, but he didn't want to give her a reason to leave. He let Noah into the house first and then retrieved his first aid kit from the bathroom.

"So, you want to tell me what happened?" Ophelia asked. She took the kit from him, and they headed into the kitchen, where the light was best. She opened the lid with a frown and removed two packets of alcohol wipes and some antibacterial cream.

"I hit someone."

Her eyes flashed in surprise. "You did?"

He rubbed the back of his neck with one hand, feeling an unexpected wave of shame. "Yeah . . ."

"Care to fill me in on the details?" She held his injured hand and carefully wiped away the blood. It stung, but he'd had worse, far worse. Her gentle fingers on his skin could have eased any pain.

"I . . ." He was going to brush it off or tell a white lie, but he decided against it. "I had a fiancée a few years back. While I was on my last tour, she slept with someone else. I just ran into the guy today at the VA center."

Ophelia stilled, her hands frozen around his. "You were engaged?"

"Yeah." He wanted to cup her chin and raise it up. He wanted her to look at him. "It was a long time ago. He was my best friend since we were teenagers. That's why I punched him."

Ophelia gently squeezed his hand before she began to spread antibacterial cream on his knuckles. "Oh God, that's awful." When she was done, he flexed his fingers. The bruises would be dark tomorrow, but he would heal. He always healed, even if it left a hell of a scar.

"Is she why you don't date anymore?" Ophelia turned away as she asked the question, and her cheeks darkened with a blush.

"She *was*." When she looked back at him, he

stared meaningfully at her. "But I was thinking of getting back out there again."

"Oh?" He could hear her faint response, and he couldn't resist smiling. This woman made him want to smile all the damn time.

"Yeah. My type, in case you're wondering, is small and curvy, with doe-brown eyes and raven-black hair."

Ophelia's lips parted, and he crowded her against the kitchen island. His hands caged her hips in, and she shivered. The clean, floral scent of her shampoo mixed with her natural feminine aroma went straight to his head. His eyes drifted along her face, from the curve of her kissable lips to the swell of her breasts beneath the tank top she wore and the gentle indentation of her collarbone.

Colt used his finger to tilt her chin up. Then he leaned down to kiss her. The second before their lips met, he felt the heady anticipation of his lips touching hers. He'd never wanted a kiss so much in his entire life. Then the distance between their mouths closed, and the world exploded in a rush of pleasure and sweetness.

The more he kissed her, the more he would crave her, but she was worth the risk. He was a man who'd fought for his country, and now he had to fight for her heart, and that was a battle he couldn't afford to lose.

od, this man . . .

    The euphoric thought drifted through Ophelia's mind as she kissed Colt back in his cozy kitchen. She thought of what he had said, how his heart had been broken and how he wanted to risk love again . . . with her. What woman would be crazy enough to turn that down? She had wanted this man from the moment she had first seen him mowing his lawn.

She curled her arms around his neck and squealed as he hoisted her up and set her down on the polished granite surface of the kitchen island. It brought her mouth level with his for deeper kisses. She spread her legs, and he stepped between them, pushing himself against her as he cradled her head while he ravaged her lips with his. His kisses were rough, hungry, unapologetic. There was nothing better than a man kissing her like he didn't care about anything else. Her last boyfriend had kissed her like he just wanted to get straight to sex, not like those kisses were fueling his passion.

Colt kissed her like he had to, like kissing her was the only thing keeping him alive. It was a rush unlike anything she'd ever experienced. Her head swam as she tried to catch her breath, and she clung to his massive shoulders.

After a few minutes, their mouths parted and he leaned back to look at her. Then he reached for the hem of her tank top and began to lift it up. His lips pursed as he took his time, forcing some control over the need she knew they were both feeling. He tossed the shirt away and gazed at her sensible bra as though she were a Victoria's Secret model.

Colt traced a finger down her chest to the edge of the bra cups before he pulled one down, exposing one breast and then the other. Her nipples pebbled in the chilled air, and he flicked one, then did the same to the other. Without a word, he bent his head and covered an aching breast with his mouth, sucking the nipple between his lips. Sharp, violent need pierced Ophelia's core, and she gasped, the sound filling the silence of the kitchen. He sucked harder, his beard brushing against her sensitive skin, tickling her.

Ophelia was incapable of speech. She could only moan and clutch Colt's head, digging her fingers into the strands of his hair and tugging in encouragement. Colt tortured each breast with pleasure until her nipples were hard and wet from his attention, and then he laid her flat on the counter. When she tried to rise, he pressed a palm on her chest, urging her back down. He unfastened her shorts and slid them off. She whimpered in anticipation as he peeled her panties off and bent between her spread thighs.

Small, hot kisses to her inner thighs were her only way of knowing what he intended before he kissed her clit, then licked her slit. She nearly bowed off the counter as she lost herself to him, to the exquisite pleasures of this man and the way he used his mouth on her. He ran his tongue over her folds, which were very wet and impossibly sensitive. She'd never been so turned on in her life. There was something about his intense sexual focus and the complete silence from him except for his hard breathing fanning over her sensitive skin. None of her fantasies had prepared her for this, not one.

He licked at her clit while he inserted one finger into her. It was tight, but it felt so good for him to enter her. She just wished it was his cock. She wriggled a little, trying to encourage more from him without using words.

Colt didn't relent. He drew a gasping climax from

her, and just as she started to come down from the rolling waves of pleasure, she felt something nudge at her entrance. She lifted her head to see that he had opened his pants and rolled a condom onto his thick shaft before starting to push into her.

Dear God, he's not going to fit. He's monstrous. He—

Colt thrust into her, feeding his cock into her inch by inch. She closed her fingers around the edge of the counter as she struggled to take him in. He was halfway inside when he thrust hard, and was fully seated inside her.

Ophelia couldn't speak. There were no words to describe the exquisite fullness. There was only him and this feeling of connection. He gazed down at her, his hazel eyes dark with lust. His hands gripped her legs, holding her thighs wide. She'd never felt more vulnerable in her life. He could fuck her ruthlessly, and she was in no position to stop him. Not that she wanted to.

Whatever Colt saw in her eyes, he seemed to see her agree to whatever he wanted. He drew in a deep breath before he began to fuck her hard. She slid on the counter, and he kept hold of her while he jackhammered into her like a man possessed. She cried out over and over, each time he filled her almost to the point of pain. Every fear, every hurt, every heartbreak from the last few months faded to nothing as Colt made love to her wildly, dangerously.

This time her orgasm was so violent, so exquisite, that she actually screamed. Colt roared in response, the sound reverberating clear through her as he unleashed all of his strength into her with a few more thrusts before everything went still. His fingers dug into her thighs, but the hold soon eased and she sank back onto the counter, too limp to move. She couldn't even lift her head to see his face.

He held still inside of her for what felt like forever, and she almost cried out when he withdrew from her body. She didn't want that connection to end. He threw the condom away and then cleaned them both with a towel before he helped her sit up. She blushed as he fixed his jeans and then cupped her face to press a slow, sweet kiss to her lips.

When they broke apart, she suddenly blurted out, "Please come over for dinner. I was planning to cook, and I want to cook for you."

For a moment, his gaze was unreadable. Then he slowly smiled. "That sounds nice. What time?"

"Uh, give me two hours?" She needed to shower, then run to the store for a few things, dress up, and cook.

"Okay. Want me to bring anything?"

She beamed at him. "No, just you." She felt ridiculously happy, and she knew she should be embarrassed, but right now that was impossible.

"All right." He helped her off the counter, and she put her clothes back on.

"Great. See you in a few hours." She kissed his cheek and rushed out of his house.

Ophelia showered, dressed, and rushed to the store to get ingredients for an instant pot barbecue beef recipe. When she got back to her car, rain was splashing in torrents down her windows. It was dark by the time she pulled into her garage.

She'd always loved storms and kept her garage door open as she unloaded the groceries from her trunk. The bags were in her arms, and she took a moment to watch the lightning illuminate the street as the rain moved in winding waves across the pavement.

She turned away, but the sight of a battered old car pulling into her driveway made her turn back. She didn't know anyone who drove a car like that, and she wasn't expecting anyone either. A chill raced down her spine, and she ran for the garage door leading into her house. She hit the button on the wall to close the garage door, but it bounced back up when the sensors were triggered by movement.

Ophelia screamed as two men rushed her in the dark. She threw the grocery bags at one man and got inside, but she couldn't get the door closed. One of them had wedged his boot in the door, and then he hit her hard in the shoulder. Pain lanced up her body as she kept trying to get the door shut.

There was a shout on the other side of the door, and suddenly it was flung wide as one of them crashed into it, sending her sprawling on her back. Her head hit the floor, and she groaned as she tried to roll over onto her hands and knees.

One of the men grabbed her head and slammed it down on the floor. "Fucking bitch!" White dots flashed in the blackness behind her eyes.

"Grab what you can and load it in the car!" the man snapped. "I'll take care of her."

Pain flowed through her as she became aware of hands gripping her wrists and dragging her along the floor into the living room. She cried out as a boot sank hard into her side. The man was kicking her, though the realization came to her through a dark, frightening tunnel that left her stunned. Why was this happening?

"Pl-please stop!" she begged.

"Shut the fuck up!" A blow smacked her face to the side, and blood filled her mouth from her split lip.

"Stop fucking around, asshole!" the other man said. "I need you to help carry the TV. It's too big."

Ophelia tried to breathe. She was being robbed. The men were using the storm to cover it up. While they were busy with the TV, she had only a minute at most to move, to get to her phone or hide. Her fuzzy mind struggled to make a decision.

Phone. Get the phone.

She crawled around the back of her couch toward the kitchen. The sounds of crashing and cursing grew distant behind her. She was going to make it. She—

"Hey, where's the bitch?"

"I don't know."

"Fucking find her!"

She heard footsteps, and suddenly strong hands grabbed her ankles.

She screamed just as a fist knocked her into terrifying nothingness.

NOAH WAS SITTING ON THE COUCH THAT BACKED UP to Colt's living room window. His tail wagged as he saw Ophelia's car pull into the driveway. Colt scratched the dog behind the ears.

"She must have made a run to the store," Colt explained to the German shepherd. The rain outside was coming down hard enough that visibility was poor. He had seen only Ophelia's car lights, but it was enough to know it was her.

Lightning flashed a moment later as an old sedan with no lights on pulled into Ophelia's driveway. Noah whined and shifted restlessly before he suddenly growled low at the back of his throat. Colt waited for the next flash of lightning, wondering who Ophelia had over. Then he saw two men run into her open garage. Every instinct warned him that Ophelia was in danger. He ran to the front door, opened it, and shouted a command at Noah.

"*Protect!*"

The dog shot out the door, and Colt was right behind him. Noah would protect Ophelia. He had been trained well with that command. God help whoever tried to hurt her now, because the dog would tear them apart.

Colt reached the garage and saw the open door into the house. Inside he heard a man scream and Noah snarling. The report of a gun made Colt flinch as he crept into the house. His breathing was fast out of fear for Ophelia, but his instincts were still good, and his fists were ready for anything. As he peered around the wall into the living room, he saw the shattered flat-screen on the floor and one man struggling with Noah. The dog had a hold on the man's arm and was hanging on for dear life.

"Shoot him, Randy!" screamed the man Noah was biting. The other man held a gun and was trying to find a way to shoot the dog to free his friend from the dog's bite, but Noah was jerking and tugging on the arm, making it hard for the second man to aim at him without shooting the first man.

"I can't! I might shoot you!"

Colt charged the man with the gun from the side and took him down like he was sacking a quarterback. They hit the ground, and the gun was knocked from the man's hand. Colt hit the man twice before the sound of Noah yelping pulled his attention away. Noah still hung on to the other man's arm, but the man held a bloody knife.

Colt surged to his feet and jumped the second robber, grabbing his wrist in one hand and his neck with the other, crashing his head against the wall. The man's eyes rolled back into his head, and he slumped to the ground.

"Release," Colt ordered the dog. Noah let go of the man's arm, and thankfully he didn't seem to be gravely injured. "Find Ophelia, Noah." The dog started sniffing, and Colt drew in a deep breath as he pulled his cell phone out and dialed 911.

"911, what's your emergency?"

"My neighbor was attacked by two men. I brought my therapy dog, and we stopped them. I need the police and an ambulance." He was breathing hard as he followed Noah into Ophelia's bedroom. He saw her legs sticking out from the other side of the bed and nearly dropped his phone as terror swept through him.

"Do you see your neighbor? Is this person hurt?"

"I just found her. Hang on." He put the phone on

speaker as he came around the bed. Ophelia was lying on her side, her hands bound with an electrical cord that had been ripped from a lamp off her nightstand. A dishcloth was stuffed into her mouth, and her face was bruised and bloody. Cuts and scratches covered her bare legs.

"Sir?" the emergency operator spoke to him.

Colt knelt and pulled the sock from her mouth, then checked for a pulse. His hand was shaking, and his blood was pounding so hard that it took a few seconds for him to calm down. Her pulse was steady but not as strong as it should be.

"My neighbor . . . she's unconscious. They bound and gagged her. They beat her bad. Please, get that ambulance here," he pleaded. Noah limped closer, sniffing at Ophelia's sandal-clad feet. He whimpered softly before he lay down.

"Police and an ambulance are on the way. What is the status of the two men who attacked your neighbor?"

"Unconscious. I'm former military. I subdued them." His tone reverted to how he would have spoken to his old commanding officer.

"Stay there. Officers are approaching the residence now." The sound of sirens grew louder. Colt remained where he was on the floor of Ophelia's bedroom, one hand on Noah's collar and the other on Ophelia's wrist to keep monitoring her pulse.

"Here!" he shouted when he heard officers calling from the doorway of the house. "We're in here!" He waited for the police to enter, the flashlights on top of their guns suddenly trained on him. He already had one hand raised. "I can't release my dog, not until he feels safe," Colt explained with a nod to the dog.

"Understood. What's your name, sir?" One of the officers approached.

"Colt Henshaw. I live next door." He slowly stood and backed away so the officer could get to Ophelia.

"Rick!" the officer shouted, looking her over. "Check to see where that ambulance is. Now."

"On it," the other officer shouted back.

"Can you tell me what happened?" the officer asked Colt.

Colt had just finished relaying the events when the EMTs arrived. They knelt by Ophelia and checked her over, then loaded her onto a stretcher and strapped her down.

"I need to go with them." He started to leave, but the officer held him back with a hand.

"We need to take a statement first."

Colt looked to the man, his hands clenching. "You can do it at the hospital. She's my girlfriend—I'm going to follow the ambulance as soon as I can get my neighbor to take my dog to the emergency vet."

The officer's eyes narrowed. "Girlfriend? You said she was your neighbor."

"She's both." He whistled to Noah, who heeled by his side as they followed the paramedics. While the EMTs prepared to put Ophelia inside the ambulance, Colt knelt and checked out Noah's injury which didn't seem that deep.

"You okay, boy?" He murmured as he gently examined the injury. Noah simply panted softly, but he didn't seem to be in a great deal of pain. Colt hated to have to choose between taking his dog to the vet and going with Ophelia, but Noah seemed in better shape.

"Colt! What happened?" Miranda ran up to him as she spotted him and Noah. He briefly told her what happened and she agreed to take Noah to the nearby emergency vet and call him as soon as the vet looked the dog over.

"Is she going to be okay?" Colt asked the paramedics as they loaded Ophelia into the ambulance. The two paramedics flashed him pitying looks.

"She's stable, but we won't know for sure until we get her to the ER." The siren started up, and Colt rushed to his truck to follow them to the hospital.

Colt had only one look at Ophelia's bruised and battered body on the gurney, and a pain far greater than any he'd ever experienced tore at his insides like a raging beast. He could lose her, when he'd finally been brave enough to open his heart.

OPHELIA CAME AWAKE IN BITS AND PIECES, drifting in and out like waves on the shore, pulling her closer to the surface. When she was finally able to open her eyes, the room was dark and hospital machines beeped softly. She didn't try to move. Something inside her knew she would hurt worse if she did. Her dry lips were cracked, and she struggled to swallow.

A figure lounged in a chair near the bed. His face was silhouetted by the moonlight coming in from the window.

"Colt . . ." Her hoarse voice sounded like she'd swallowed gravel and it hurt to speak. Colt stirred awake and glanced at her. His eyes widened.

"Ophelia." That single utterance, so full of hope and worry, dug into her heart.

"Water?" she asked.

He got up and picked up her plastic water mug and held it to her lips. She drank a little before he set the mug down and reached up to stroke her hair, only to freeze in place.

"God, I'm afraid to touch you," he murmured.

"What happened?" Memories of what had happened were still fuzzy and came more in flashes than clear pictures.

"Two men followed you into your house. I saw

them go into the garage. When Noah and I got there, they'd already hurt you. I'm so sorry, sweetheart. I should have been there." He looked devastated, as if he were somehow responsible. Pain created black shadows in his eyes.

"What happened to the men?"

"Arrested. Both of them. The police suspect they're responsible for half a dozen home invasions in the area."

She closed her eyes for a moment. "Good."

"The hospital performed a rape kit," he said quietly. "I had to tell them we were dating and that we had sex earlier that day. Do you remember if they hurt you that way?"

She shook her head. She only remembered trying to crawl to the phone.

"The doctor doesn't think they did, but we weren't sure if you remembered anything. I was positive I got to them before anything happened, but . . ."

"Colt . . ." She didn't know what she wanted to say. She was so tired and still in pain.

"God, Ophelia, I'm so damn sorry."

"It's not your fault." She started to close her eyes. "I'm tired and need to rest."

Colt started to stand. "I'll go, then."

"No, please stay."

He moved his chair closer to the bed and laced

his fingers with hers. It was like a lifeline in the dark storm of her body's pain.

"I'll stay."

"Thank you."

She managed a weak smile as she drifted off to sleep. She thought—or perhaps dreamed—that he said he loved her.

5

Ophelia peered out of the window of Colt's truck as he pulled into her driveway. After a week in the hospital she was finally home, and God, it felt good not to have to spend another night in a stiff hospital bed. Noah sat between her and Colt, his tongue lolling out as he watched his owner open the driver's-side door. The shepherd had a bandage around his upper leg and a few minor stitches, but like Colt had hoped, the dog's injury had been more of a glancing scrape than a serious injury. Ophelia rested one hand on the dog's shoulders.

"Noah, out." Colt stepped out of the truck, and the shepherd leapt past him onto the ground. Ophelia opened her door, but before she could get down, Colt was there with his hands on her hips as he gently set her on her feet.

Despite his gruff demeanor, he was always such a gentleman around her. It was so sweet and sexy at the same time. She hated to admit it—it always felt like she had to hand in her feminist card when she thought along these lines—but she liked it when Colt opened a door for her. It felt respectful, and she liked that in a man. Even her last boyfriend had always been a gentleman. But Colt had taken it to a whole new level while he'd cared for her in the hospital.

"You know I can walk, right?" she teased.

"I know." The sudden tenderness in Colt's gaze stilled her heart. "I just like to get my hands on you whenever I can."

"Oh? In that case, maybe I can't walk so well."

"Ophelia!" Miranda rushed across the street to greet them. "Oh, honey, you look so much better." She gave Ophelia a gentle hug. "The gals will be thrilled to know that you're home." Miranda then looked to Colt. "Thank you for taking care of our girl." She hugged the big, gruff Navy SEAL and shot Ophelia a wink.

"I don't mind. She's not *too* high maintenance," Colt said with a straight face.

"High maintenance, huh?" Ophelia replied. "And to think, I had dreamed up some great ways to pay you back for such dedicated attention."

His way of keeping her distracted from the pain of recovering had been by telling her all the dirty fantasies he'd had about her between that first kiss and when they'd finally made love. She'd never been so excited to get home in her life, because she didn't plan on waiting a second longer to to be alone with him.

Now she had his full attention, and his eyes glowed with desire. "Oh? Care to share any, sweetheart?"

"I better let you two settle in. I'll see you tomorrow night for drinks." Miranda smirked. "Assuming you can walk."

Ophelia blushed. "Thanks, Miranda." In the past week, Colt had made it very clear that they were officially dating, and she'd heard from nearly every one of the women who lived on their quiet little street once word spread. One group text with Miranda, Jennifer, and Eliza had been filled with dozens of completely inappropriate questions, which she had read aloud to Colt. It had made her laugh, even though that had hurt her ribs, and he'd sat there frowning and grumbling about women, margaritas, and bikinis in the most adorable way.

Colt put a gentle arm around her waist. "Let's go inside and continue this discussion." The second she entered her house, she stiffened as she searched for signs of blood and broken glass, or any evidence of what had happened. There was no hint of the epic struggle that had occurred.

"You okay?" Colt asked as he held her close.

"Yeah. I just expected to see the mess, you know?"

"I had a few friends come in and fix everything while you were in the hospital."

"Even the TV?" She saw a TV sitting on the stand, ready to be turned on. She thought the robbers had broken it.

"No, I bought you a new one. Hope you don't mind." He was watching her with increased concern.

"No, I don't, but I insist on paying you back for that." She realized it was actually bigger than her old TV. "How many inches is that? Mine was forty-two inches . . ."

He looked at his boots like a guilty schoolboy. "Er . . . sixty-five? I just figured that if I was going to be spending time over here, we should have a bigger screen."

She couldn't deny that she liked the sound of *we* when he said it like that.

"I really do have to pay you back for that." She was going to insist on it.

"Okay, I'll let you," he said carefully. "But you're welcome to see it as a get-well gift."

Ophelia stared around the room for a long moment, letting the awful memories wash over her. The trauma therapist at the hospital had told her to relive the attack and, more importantly, relive the surviving of it. She gently pulled free of Colt and walked through the living room to her bedroom. She had only dim memories of Colt speaking to her, touching her, and the paramedics shining a bright light into her pupils. Colt had held her hand the entire time.

Noah walked ahead of Ophelia with a slight limp in his front right leg. Ophelia felt forever bound to the big dog for rushing in so fearlessly to defend her. He had saved her life.

Next week she would face the two men who'd attacked her at their arraignment hearing. She wanted to look them both in the eyes and let them see that she was not afraid of them.

Ophelia's gaze went to the spot on the floor in her bedroom where she'd been found, and then she looked to Colt as he filled the doorway. God, he was gorgeous, and he was all hers. That fact still made her smile, and she held out a hand to him.

"You okay?"

"Yes. I was just reliving the incident, remembering that you and Noah saved me. I'm alive and well, thanks to you both."

He gathered her in his arms, and she buried her face against his throat. She had no desire to move from his arms, and if she could have, she would have stayed there forever.

"Do you want me to stay with you tonight?" he asked. He pressed his lips to the crown of her hair. "I can stay on the couch."

"Yes, I'd like that, but you won't be on the couch." The soft press of their bodies reminded her of how much she wanted him. It had been a cruel twist of fate that she'd had one day with him before being hurt so badly in the attack.

She lifted her head. "Colt?"

He looked down at her, one hand threaded through her hair in a way that felt wonderful. "Hmm?" He was always doing that, finding sweet little ways to keep his hands on her. She felt loved. She felt *desired*.

"Will you take me to bed?"

"Sweetheart, I don't think—"

"Just go slow and I'll be okay. Please. I just need to be with you."

His warm hazel eyes were shrouded with uncertainty and his dark hair feel across his forehead making him look bashful and charming in a way she'd never expected from her fierce neighbor. She bit her bottom lip and looked up at him. "Don't make me beg."

"But I don't want to hurt you."

"You won't—I'm a tough cookie."

"That you are. Should we go to my house?" He looked to the spot where he'd found her on the floor.

"No, here. I want to replace the bad memories with good ones."

"Okay, but if you need to stop at any time, you tell me."

He pulled off his shirt, and she slipped out of her sandals. Ophelia unbuttoned her blouse and slipped out of her shorts and panties, then removed her bra as he finished kicking off his boots, socks, and jeans. She sat on the bed completely naked, and he joined her. His gaze swept over her, his desire making his eyes as warm as melted honey.

"You're so beautiful and so brave. You know that, don't you?" He cupped the back of her head for a slow, deep kiss that made her toes curl.

"Am I?" she asked. She traced his collarbone with her fingers, and his lips curved into a smile that was half hidden beneath his beard.

"Braver than anyone I know."

He leaned in to kiss her again, and the sweetness of that kiss burned her in the best way. She was wild for Colt, more than any man she'd ever been with, and yet it wasn't just desire she felt. She had a feeling that the quiet, calm depths of her affection for him was something infinitely more, like love. For too long she'd been letting herself live a reserved life, even with the men in her past relationships. Now, she did indeed feel brave.

"Colt." She curled her arms around his neck and pulled him down so he covered her body with his.

"Yeah?" He swept his eyes over her with a wistful expression as he cupped her face. His thumb brushed over her cheek as she parted her thighs and he settled between them.

"I think I'm falling in love with you."

There, she'd done it. She'd exposed herself and left her heart wide open.

"I think I am too, with you," he replied, his voice a little rough. "I didn't want to, not after my last relationship, but I couldn't help myself. And I don't regret that for a minute." His body heat seeped into her, and she wound her arms around his back, holding him close as he kissed her again.

They made love, slow and tender and yet with intensity and passion. Ophelia felt a radiant light glowing inside her. Their breaths mixed in silent intimacy, broken only by soft sighs and the sound of their skin sliding against the sheets. Even being gentle, Colt still managed to overwhelm her with his sensual intensity. He left no part of her unexplored, no part of her unkissed. She giggled as he searched for the ticklish spots behind her knees and just below her arms along her sides. His responding chuckle of delight to her reactions was music to her ears. It was a gift to have a partner to share sweet moments like this with. She'd always wanted that but had never truly experienced it before.

When he finally entered her, she was trembling with need and quiet euphoria. This was no frantic coupling. It was measured and slow, but no less powerful than the first time they had come together.

Colt pinned her hands in the bedding and rode her body slowly, holding her gaze as he filled her deeply with each thrust. He stole a kiss every few seconds, but he seemed determined not to look away as her climax hit. Her toes curled and her back arched as the orgasm scorched clear down to her soul. Colt's body tensed as he spilled himself inside her. After that, they stayed connected a long moment, both lost in the intense moment of true oneness, neither of them wanting to let go of it first.

Ophelia looked up at him, her body lax as she coaxed him to lie down beside her. Then she nestled up against him. Everything terrible that had happened in this room lost its hold over her. There was only this peaceful joy, this sense of connectedness to Colt. She had some regrets in life, of course, but none with him. And that was all that mattered.

One month later

Colt was strangely nervous as he parked his truck in the VA lot. Noah and Ophelia were with him. It was the first time he'd brought Ophelia here, and he wondered what she would think. Seeing wounded veterans could be hard on some people, and in some cases it didn't affect a person at all, which was somehow worse.

He wasn't testing Ophelia, not exactly, but he did need to see how she handled his world. He and Noah belonged with the veterans, and helping them mattered. Any woman he wanted to spend the rest of his life with would need to understand this part of him, as well as the wounded men and women who'd served this country.

"You ready?" he asked her.

"Of course." She handed him Noah's leash, and they headed for the entrance. The usual gathering was in the lobby, waiting for Noah to arrive at his expected time.

"They're really all here for him?" Ophelia asked.

"They are. When we serve in dangerous locations, we have trained working dogs with us. I can't quite put it into words, but a dog makes you feel like you're home. Safe. It makes the soldiers feel more connected—to the dog, the mission, and each other. When they see Noah here—I don't know, it just helps the emotional healing somehow." His throat constricted as he explained. He'd always known it in his gut, but he'd never been able to put it into words until now.

"It's incredible." Ophelia's tone was one of genuine pride. Ever since the attack, she'd lost all fear of Noah, and he'd taken to following her around whenever he wasn't under orders to stay put. Their unlikely alliance had Colt smiling.

"Well hello there, stranger." Nancy walked over to him. "I thought you'd forgotten all about us."

"Not in a million years," said Colt.

Her eyes lit up when she saw Ophelia. "Is this who I think it is?"

"Nancy, this is Ophelia. Ophelia, this is Nancy."

Ophelia smiled. "It's so nice to meet you. Did you serve with Colt?"

"No, but we've known each other for a couple of years now. Ever since he started coming to the center."

"I didn't know he's been coming here that long." Ophelia looked to him in amazement.

"Yeah, he started coming here almost the day he moved in." Nancy nudged Colt playfully.

"It felt a bit like home being around the other vets," Colt explained. "I didn't feel the need to hide or put up barriers." He couldn't believe he was admitting that to Ophelia, but he wanted her to know why this place mattered to him.

Nancy caught a passing veteran with a wave. "Hey,

Jeremy, why don't you introduce Ophelia to the guys?" Ophelia left with Jeremy, holding Noah's leash, to meet Colt's friends.

"So, let's hear it." Nancy looked at him expectantly.

"Hear what?"

"Admit it—I was right. You took my advice and got back into the game. And damn, honey, you did good. She's as sweet and adorable as you said." Nancy patted his arm.

Colt smiled. "She's also brave as fucking hell. She was attacked in a home invasion a month ago. Almost died, but she came back even stronger. She's not even bitter. She's like a breath of fresh air, but . . . like air I can't live without. That doesn't make sense, does it?"

Nancy's eyes softened. "Sure it does. You love her, simple as that."

"I do. I think I fell in love with her from the start, but when she was lying in that hospital bed, I realized I was *all in* for her."

"*All in* is good." Nancy gave him a push. "You better go rescue your girl before all those handsome soldiers start hitting on her."

Colt joined Ophelia, who was talking to the vets and asking them about their families and their interests and how their recovery was going. She fit so perfectly into his life. He never imagined that he would feel that way after Talia, but with Ophelia it was simple. He loved her. She loved him. Everything else was just details.

When they were done and leaving the center, Ophelia slid her hand into his. Noah trotted at their side as they walked back to the truck.

"You didn't mind seeing the vets?"

"No. They're amazing, like you." She smiled. "Speaking of vets, my dad wants to meet you and see the center, if that's okay. He and my mom are coming to visit next weekend."

Colt chuckled. "Sure. After my three tours overseas, I think I can face a protective dad, so long as you're at my side."

She giggled. "I told him he has to behave, since I'm crazy in love with you."

Colt stopped her, pinning her against the side of his truck and stealing a kiss. "I'm crazy in love with you too. You *devastate* me, sweetheart."

"I hope that's a good thing." She snuggled against him, kissing his neck before pulling his head down for a deep, lingering kiss.

"Oh, it's a very good thing," he said as he captured her mouth again. This woman was the answer to every question he might have for the universe. She was his future, his life, and he couldn't wait to start living again.

. . .

THANK YOU SO MUCH FOR READING *DEVASTATE Me*! I hope you enjoyed Colt and Ophelia's story! Hungry for another delicious alpha male romance?

Check out my novel *Love in the Wild: A Tarzan Retelling* where Eden, a photographer stumbles upon the discovery of a lifetime in Uganda when a wild jungle god of a man rescues her. Get the book HERE! Or Turn the page to read a 3 chapter sneak peek!

A TARZAN RETELLING
LOVE
IN THE
Wild
EMMA CASTLE

LOVE IN THE WILD
PROLOGUE

Uganda- Present Day

"Get on your knees," a cold voice commanded.

Eden Matthews sank to her knees. Half a dozen men and women next to her did the same. One woman was sobbing, and a man was begging for his life. But Eden saw no mercy in the eyes of the man who stood in front of her holding a gun to her head.

All around them the jungle was quiet. Even the animals and insects seemed to have sensed the danger and elected to stay still. She stared at the barrel of the gun, her gaze fixed on the circular black hole, then forced herself to look her soon-to-be-murderer in the eyes. The man was unshaven, mid-forties, his clothing splattered with blood and mud. Behind him were four other men with stony, empty black eyes, all armed. They were a mix of white and black men, and the heavy weapons they carried meant they were most likely rebels. Or worse—poachers.

"We were supposed to be safe," one woman whispered to herself. "This is a national park. We have permits . . ."

Permits didn't matter to men like these—these were the true monsters of the jungle.

"Keep your mouths shut," the leader snapped. She didn't dare take her eyes away from him. His gun swung a few inches to Eden's left at the older woman who'd spoken.

Eden's heart was beating so fast she was amazed she hadn't had a heart attack. These men wouldn't let them go. They were going to kill them and leave their bodies in the Ugandan jungle, never to be found. The gorillas she had come to photograph had fled before these men had arrived, as if they had sensed the danger. If they were poachers, and the gorillas had been their intended target, Eden at least hoped the majestic creatures were far away and safe.

"Cash, what we gonna do with them, eh?" one of the men asked their leader.

"Shut up—I'm thinking," he growled. His eyes swept over the group of visitors and their two Ugandan guides.

"The boss wouldn't like witnesses," the other man added.

"True." The one called Cash stroked his beard, and then, with terrifying slowness, he swept the gun to the forehead of the man at the far end of the tourist group and fired. Eden jerked as his body fell face-first onto the leaf-covered ground.

Several more bangs echoed in the small clearing, and more bodies fell.

Eden wasn't able to close her eyes. Fear had so immobilized her that she simply couldn't move, couldn't breathe. She could only watch.

"Maybe we keep one alive?" Cash volunteered to his men with a cruel laugh. "These other bitches were old. But this one, she's fresh and young. We can have our fun with her first. The boss would never need to know."

Lungs burning, Eden sucked in a breath, her back aching from being stiff on her knees.

"Yes, I think we'll keep her." Cash lowered his gun, but Eden didn't relax. Whatever hell was about to come next for her would be far, far worse than a quick death.

Blood roared in her ears, so loud that the trees actually seemed to tremble and the ground to vibrate.

Wait, no. That sound wasn't in her head. It was coming from somewhere else, somewhere distant, but near enough to frighten the men closest to her.

"What the fuck was that?" Cash demanded.

"*Mnyama*," one of the men murmured in Swahili. "*Mnyama Anakuja!*"

Eden didn't speak much Swahili, but it sounded like he said, *The beast is coming.*

"A silverback?" Cash asked.

The man shook his head. "No. The pale ghost."

"Pale ghost? What the fuck are you talking about?"

Two of the men exchanged glances and just ran. They vanished into the moss-covered hagenia trees that formed the canopies high above them.

Cash spun around, firing shots in their direction before he turned back toward Eden. The roar echoed again, sending birds into flight and small monkeys in the trees scampering away.

"We should go!"

The other men clambered away at once, but Cash shouted at them. "Not until I kill this one." He pointed his gun at her again.

Eden closed her eyes tight. She imagined her parents' faces back in Arkansas, could see the door of her childhood home. She choked down her despair and longing to be there in that moment and not here —anywhere but here.

The gun went off. Eden experienced a second of stunned surprised because she still felt the jungle air thick with moisture and smelled the heavy scent of sweat around her. She was dead, so why did she still smell the jungle?

"Ah!" Cash's scream came a millisecond later, followed by a sickening crunch.

Eden didn't dare open her eyes as she heard the sounds of violence—screams and snapping bones.

The beast was here. Her stomach churned as she swallowed down the rise of bile in her throat and her breath escaped in rapid pants of terror. She would be next. The long silence that followed made her brave enough to open her eyes, slowly taking in the scene of carnage. Cash lay dead a dozen feet away, his neck twisted right around. That was something.

The other tourists she had come with were all dead, but they had been left untouched by the beast. She swallowed hard as tears blurred her vision.

The sound of footsteps behind her and a huffing noise caused her to flinch and close her eyes again. Body heat and hot breath on the back of her neck sent a chill down her spine and stirred her hair. The beast was still here. She was next.

Please, let it kill me quickly.

A grunting noise, similar to the ones made by the gorillas, came from behind her. Something touched her ponytail. She gasped and threw herself to the ground on pure instinct, her hands crunching into the leaves beneath her. The beast moved somewhere in front of her. When she dared to look, her lips parted but no sound escaped.

A man crouched in front of her, ten feet away. His tan skin was covered with blackened, drying mud, making him look more monster than man. His long dark hair hung in loose tendrils down around his shoulders. His eyes were a vivid dark blue, and they narrowed on her as his full lips pressed into a hard frown.

In one hand the man held a blade. His other hand was curled into a fist. She watched the corded muscles of his forearm ripple as he shifted and moved. There was a lithe grace to his nearly naked body as he shifted back and forth on his bare feet. A loincloth of animal skin covered his groin but left his legs bare to her view. He chuffed at her softly, like a jaguar. But the strangest thing, perhaps, was a band of gold that rested on his brow like a crown, the precious metal shaped into small leaves like a laurel wreath.

He gestured with his balled fist to the man on the ground and grunted again.

Eden blinked, unsure what to do or say. This man had saved her. But who was he? Where had he come from? Why was he grunting instead of speaking?

"Hi," she whispered, and he halted in his gestures. "Do you understand me?"

The man tilted his head to the side, and his

nostrils flared. It was hard to read his face with the mud streaked across it.

"Hello?" She tried to greet him again. The word *hello* was also used in Swahili, in case he spoke that rather than English.

He slowly straightened to a towering height, and she got to her feet as well. Eden kept her distance, not knowing what to expect with this wild man.

She tried some Swahili and continued to stare at him. "*Kiswahili?*"

Suddenly his head turned, and he scanned the forest. It was still eerily quiet. Eden knew his attention was focused elsewhere, yet she had a sense he had missed nothing, including her movements. The man threw his head back and let out a roar, the same roar that had sent Cash's Ugandan men running for the hills. They had known the danger of whoever this man was.

She asked him if he spoke Swahili. "*Unaongea Kiswahili?*" Unfortunately, she didn't know enough of the language to truly have a conversation.

Her savior shot her another distracted look before he grunted again at the forest and whistled sharply. There was an answering whistle far to her left. The man turned her way, and with lightning-quick reflexes, he grabbed her.

Eden screamed, but a second later the air was knocked from her lungs as he threw her over his shoulder. He began to run, dodging through the trees and leaping over the taller bushes and vegetation like an Olympic hurdler. The impact of his feet jarred her and sent a punch to her stomach. She was going to throw up if he kept this up much longer.

Where was he going? What was he going to do to her? Why didn't he communicate? He acted . . . well, he acted more like an animal than a person. A wild man. It made no sense.

Eventually he stopped running. He rolled her off his shoulder and onto the ground. She couldn't stop it —her stomach emptied its contents, and she lay gasping on the ground at the base of a particularly thick-rooted hagenia tree. She clawed at the ground, trying to catch her breath and stop the shaking of her arms and legs.

Her head spun, and she gazed up at the distant light, barely able to make it out through the trees above. She saw something jutting from the base of the tree, going all the way up. Small pieces of wood, like tiny steps in the trunk, created a path all the way up the tree. The wild man grasped her hand and pulled her to her feet. He then gestured for her to climb onto his back. Was he kidding?

She shook her head violently. "No, no, I'm not—"

He lunged for her, and she shrieked, holding up her hands.

"Okay!"

He pointed at his back, and he faced the tree, waiting patiently.

It was weird climbing onto this stranger's back, but she did it. He used the wooden steps the way a mountain climber would use footholds. She nearly closed her eyes as they reached ten feet and kept on going. The tops of the trees looked to be another ten or fifteen feet away.

As they reached the heavy foliage above, the man pushed upward, and the foliage moved away in a nearly perfect square shape, just large enough to accommodate their two bodies. He continued to climb, and Eden gasped.

The tree went up another fifteen feet, through a hole in the roof that was sealed with mud. All around them was wood—chopped timbers worn smooth into planks, forming a structure around her and the man like a tree house.

A tree house? Here?

He crawled across the floor and tapped her legs. She slowly let go and touched her feet down. The wooden floor was as solid as a rock. Eden stared around at the tree house. It had to have been built nearly twenty feet off the ground. The bottom of it was completely camouflaged from below.

"What is this place?" she asked, mostly to herself. She saw a wooden door with a simple flipped latch made with thick rope. A small window-like opening allowed for some minimal light.

The man grunted at her and pointed to a corner of the little structure. Eden saw nothing there. The man moved toward her, and she immediately backed into the corner he pointed to. She fell back, landing on her bottom, and he held up a palm and made that soft chuffing noise again. Did he want her to stay there? He opened the trapdoor and started to climb down the way they had come up.

"Wait! Where are you going?" She started to move, but he grunted and huffed at her, and she halted. He pointed to the corner, and she shifted back to the corner wall, clutching her camera to her chest. He gazed at her a long moment, those blue eyes solid and inscrutable as he watched her. Then he disappeared from view, pulling the trapdoor down behind him.

Eden wasn't sure how long she sat there staring at the door. After what felt like forever, her muscles relaxed and the tension in her body slowed and seeped out of her. She slumped onto the floor on her side. Her body trembled, and a rush of tears came hard. She cried as the recent events all came back to her. The dead faces of the men and women who'd traveled deep into the impenetrable forest with her. Everyone eager for the experience of a lifetime.

Sweet Maggie, humorous Harold, and all the

others whom she'd formed a bond with in so short a time. All dead. Their lives had been snuffed out because they had been in the wrong place at the wrong time.

And what about her? She was alive, but was she ever going to get out of the jungle? And who was the beast of the forest who'd saved her? Who was the pale ghost?

CHAPTER 1
TWENTY-TWO YEARS AGO

Amelia Haywood sat in the small Cessna, her tiny son, Thorne, in the seat beside her.

She grinned and pointed at the dense miles of spreading Ugandan forest far below them. "See? Look at the jungle." Thorne squirmed and stretched up in his seat to peer out the oval window. Amelia stroked a hand down his dark hair. It was silky as a baby's, even though Thorne was three years old as of last week.

Thorne pointed a tiny finger at the window. "Mummy!"

"Yes, Thorne, that's the jungle."

"Monkey!" He looked down at the child's picture book in his lap, where it said, *M is for monkey.* Then he focused back on the window.

"Jacob, how much farther is it?" Amelia asked her husband.

Jacob turned to face her from the seat next to the pilot. His dark hair and vivid blue eyes were a mirror image of their son's. Thorne looked like her a little too, around the mouth, especially when he smiled. That pleased Amelia, because Jacob always said it was her smile that he dreamed about whenever he closed his eyes. Amelia had never imagined she could love someone as much as her husband, but she did. Jacob and Thorne were her entire world.

"We've got about another hour until we get to the airstrip," Jacob guessed.

Charlie, their hired pilot, nodded. "He's right, about an hour."

"Tomorrow we'll see the monkeys," Amelia said to her son. She turned the book's pages until she got to the letter *G*. A picture of a gorilla was below the letter.

"Gorilla." She spoke the word slowly and clearly.

Thorne planted his palm on the picture and said loudly, "Monkey!"

"Gorilla," she said again.

The child turned serious eyes to hers and then said, "Go-willa."

"Close enough." Amelia chuckled and reached up to finger the necklace at her throat. It was a small gold chain with a gold ginkgo leaf. Jacob had given it to her on the night he proposed. She'd gotten a ring, of course, a lovely princess cut diamond that was a family heirloom, but Jacob had said he wanted to give her a gift that was special, and this most certainly was.

From the beginning she and Jacob had been a perfect match, both in love with wildlife and conservation. Because of his family's wealth, they had been able to build a center near Bwindi Impenetrable Forest for park guides and guests to rest and relax before making the trek into the woods to see the gorillas.

They had also donated a large sum of money to support anti-deforestation efforts and a police force to protect the shrinking population of mountain gorillas. For the first time since she had been pregnant with Thorne, they were able to return to Africa, the cradle of civilization.

For as long as Amelia could remember, she had felt a pull to this beautiful continent. It was one of the few places that still held mysteries unseen by human eyes. It wasn't a desert plain—it was mountainous, with depressions and shallow lakes, waterfalls, and rivers.

Amelia had studied the varied geography on the continent while at university. The mountains fed the major rivers, causing the waterways to bleed into undulating savannas until they fell in a series of rapids and waterfalls into narrow gorges and coastal plains.

The rivers themselves were not navigable for any great distance. Travelers, traders, soldiers, and explorers from ancient times to present day had all failed to penetrate the interior heart of Africa.

Amelia could feel that heart beating, steady as a drum, calling her to come closer, to seek out answers deep in the misty mountains. Legends were born and made here. Amelia wanted to be among them, to explore and discover, conserve and protect.

Thorne continued to turn the pages of the book, speaking the words softly to himself in his toddler voice that was sometimes more gibberish than real words. He was a quiet child. He spoke little, but she knew he was smart. He was already learning to recognize the letters and their sounds, and he was even sounding out a few simple words in his picture books.

The plane suddenly dropped a little. Amelia's heart jumped in her chest, but then she chuckled. Thorne squealed in delight.

"Heavens, what's the matter, Charlie? You didn't let Jacob take over flying, did you?"

Charlie held tight to the controls. "No, we seem to have hit a draft."

The plane jerked, and Amelia checked her seat belt and Thorne's, making sure they were secure.

"Are you buckled in?" Jacob called back to them.

"Yes."

"Good. Hold on—"

The plane's engine suddenly sputtered, and the plane tipped down. The engine reengaged for a brief few seconds before giving out again. But it was too late. The plane dropped out of the sky toward the jungle below.

The next few seconds happened in flashes. *Smoke—screams—plummeting—trees—crash—silence.*

⛧

AMELIA COUGHED AS SHE WOKE IN THE THICK darkness. For a second, she couldn't remember what had happened. She strained to see anything as her eyes adjusted to the dark. A soft whimper beside her made her flinch.

"Mummy . . ." Thorne's voice came from somewhere beside her.

"Hold on, darling," she said and unfastened her seat belt. The inside of the Cessna was becoming clearer as her eyes adjusted to the darkness. They must have landed below the canopy of hagenia trees.

She unclipped Thorne's seat belt and felt around his tiny face. "Are you hurt, my love?" she asked, searching for any injury. He shook his head.

"Jacob! Charlie!" she called out.

There was a cough at the front of the plane. "Darling?" Jacob's voice, rusty sounding, came back to her.

"Charlie?" she called out again, but no sound came from the pilot's chair. A massive tree had pierced the window between the two seats in the front of the plane.

Her husband reached over and clapped a hand on Charlie's shoulder, giving the man a gentle shake. He didn't respond. Jacob picked up the man's wrist and put two fingers against his skin.

"No pulse," Jacob said. He turned Charlie's head slightly, exposing the part of his skull that had been caved in by the tree limb. "Christ . . ." Jacob closed his eyes briefly and exhaled a heavy sigh.

Amelia covered her mouth with her hands as grief squeezed her heart. *Poor Charlie.*

Jacob unclipped his belt and climbed through the narrow aisle over fallen luggage toward them. "Are you and Thorne okay?"

"Yes, we're all right." She pulled Thorne onto her lap. "What happened?"

"The engine gave out." Jacob ruffled a hand through Thorne's hair and kissed Amelia on the forehead. "Thank Christ you're all right."

Jacob turned to the door on the side of the plane and twisted the handle. After a few seconds it groaned and gave way. A wave of heat and humid air filled the cabin. Jacob stuck his head out into the jungle.

"I think we're still a long way from the airstrip. It looks like the plane made it all the way to the ground, but we won't have to worry about it being unstable if we move about the cabin." He pulled his head back inside and glanced around. "Look for the first aid kit. There might be a flare gun and some supplies."

Amelia tucked their son back into his seat and helped Jacob search the cabin.

"At least we have food," she said. They had brought a few weeks' worth of provisions. She had insisted on having dried edibles packed on the plane before they left London.

"I found the satellite phone," Jacob said with a relieved sigh. "I'll call Cameron." He dialed his younger brother's number back in London.

"Damn. It went to voice mail," he muttered. "Cameron, it's Jacob. Our plane crashed somewhere west of the Bwindi airstrip. I need you to call the number of the forest guides that I sent you in an email last week. Have them start looking for us right away. Make sure—" Jacob stopped abruptly. "Bloody hell."

"What's wrong?"

"The message shut off." He ended the call and turned off the phone to preserve the battery.

Amelia located the first aid kit and Jacob's handgun, which was safe in its case with a box of ammunition.

"I want us to sleep inside the plane. It's the safest place. I'm going to move Charlie's body outside and bury him, if I can. When they find us, we can retrieve his remains then. I'll find the multitool. It should have a pickax on one end."

Amelia nodded in agreement. She didn't like thinking about Charlie's body being out there where it might attract animals and insects, but they had to stay safe. A corpse close to them would only increase the risk of predators, not to mention infection and disease.

"Let me help you." Amelia checked to make sure Thorne was in his seat. She cupped his face and gazed into his big blue eyes. "Stay here, honey. Mummy and Daddy will be right back."

She joined Jacob at the front of the plane. The cockpit window was smashed into fractured pieces like frosted glass. Charlie's limp body sagged back in the seat, and Jacob leaned forward and hugged him as he lifted him up. Then he moved the body toward her. Amelia shivered as she took the man's wrists and backed her way out of the plane's door. She and Jacob carried the pilot a good distance from the plane, but they kept the plane in their sight as they laid him down.

Jacob dragged his fingers through his dark hair

and met Amelia's gaze. "We can't dig a deep grave, not without shovels. The small ax will have to be enough. It has a sharp-edged scoop on the other end."

Amelia had no words. It was an unspeakable tragedy to leave their pilot's body to the elements and wild animals, but what choice did they have?

She reached out and clasped her husband's hand and squeezed it. "I'm sorry, Jacob." She could see the pain in his eyes. He was a man with a heart deeper than the ocean. He loved all living things and valued all life.

Jacob led her away from Charlie's body back to the plane. They stopped just outside the cabin, listening to the cadence of the jungle, the hum and chirp of insects, the blend of wild, exotic birds and monkeys, oblivious to the disaster that had just happened. Jacob and Amelia exchanged a long, meaningful glance. It was as if the jungle was beginning to swallow the plane and the three surviving passengers whole.

Jacob gently gripped her hips, pulling her to him, and she wound her arms around his neck. He embraced her, hugging her to him, and brushed his hand up and down her back.

"We're going to get through this. Cameron knows were alive. He won't stop looking for us. Until then, we can have a proper family adventure. Just think:

Lofty and Cameron would have a good laugh if they were here with us."

Amelia chuckled shakily. "Lofty thinks everything is an adventure." She thought of Jacob's old schoolmate, the Earl of Lofthouse, whom everyone called Lofty, and the idea did give her a bit of spark back. Lofty was a delightful man with a sense of humor and a taste for expensive brandy. He, Cameron, and Jacob had been thick as thieves as boys.

She nodded. He was trying to keep things light, but emotions rolled through her like a building storm. Her husband and child were in an ancient forest, possibly unreachable for any rescue, and she didn't know how to protect them. Danger was everywhere.

THE NEXT TWO WEEKS OF LIVING IN THE DOWNED plane were not easy. Jacob Haywood kept a close eye on his wife and child, making sure they were safe at all times.

He also purified their water from a nearby river by mixing it with a solution that contained iodine and chlorine dioxide tablets, which killed off some giardia parasites. Thorne always made a face when he had to drink the tablet-treated water, but he would look at Jacob, and with a little weary sigh he would drink the water. The boy never complained, even when his small belly grumbled with hunger. Most days Jacob felt like a failure. He and Amelia both had staved off eating whenever possible to give more food to their son, but it was time he started trying to hunt. Uganda had an antelope species called the kob, which lived in these forests. With any luck he could find some, or fish in the river that he'd found not too far from them.

"Darling?" Jacob retrieved his gun from the case inside the cockpit where he'd hidden it out of Thorne's sight for safety.

Amelia was sitting in one of the seats with Thorne, reading the jungle alphabet book to him. "Yes?"

"I'm going to go hunting, and maybe I'll fish in the river. Stay here with Thorne. I should be back in a few hours."

She stood and lifted Thorne into her arms. "Jacob, I don't know if that's safe."

He was almost too big to hold like that, but Jacob had the sudden urge to have his child in his arms. He held out his hands, and Amelia passed him the toddler. Thorne rested his cheek on Jacob's shoulder as he cradled the boy, pressing his own cheek on the child's head.

A realization dawned on him as he swayed the little boy in his arms. Someday he would be holding

Thorne for the last time. At some point the boy would be too big, too old for this. Was *this* the last time? Would Jacob even be aware of it when that last time he held his son came and went? A chill crept along his arms and the back of his neck. It felt like someone had stepped over his grave.

He held Thorne a moment longer before he gave him back to his wife. Amelia offered him a wistful smile, but her eyes were heavy with concern.

"I'll be back soon," he promised and kissed her quick and hard.

"Be careful," Amelia warned as he stepped into the jungle that awaited him outside the security of the downed Cessna.

The trek into the jungle took nearly an hour. He glimpsed a few simian-shaped shadows above him, swinging or jumping between the trees. But he didn't aim his gun at them. He knew the dangers of ingesting monkey meat, so he would only kill them as a last resort. He climbed over the rocks, wound his way through tightly growing moss-covered trees, and chopped down thick vegetation with a machete they had brought along on the plane.

He was nearly at the river—it was only another quarter of a mile—when he heard something moving through the brush. There were some low-level foothills that had caves nearby. He had discovered a cave a week ago but hadn't gone too far in. Ebola was often found in African caves. He didn't want to risk contracting that virus.

Whatever was heading toward the cave was definitely big. It might be a kob. He abandoned his path toward the river and followed the sound at a safe distance.

When the sounds ahead of him stopped near the black cavernous entrance to the cave, he halted, holding his breath, but a second later, he exhaled in a rush as he heard human voices.

"This is the one, Holt," a man said. "I saw the gold myself."

Gold? Jacob wondered how they had found gold here.

"Bloody natives," one man grumbled. "Burying gold in a bleedin' cave. What's the point of it? Well, get to work. I want to see it."

Jacob peeled a branch out of the way of his face and saw a group of men entering the cave. They didn't look friendly. The guns they were carrying and their general unkempt appearance, added to their talk of hidden gold, made them dangerous. They were not the sort of men Jacob could ask for help.

He slowly backed away, but not before he saw one man emerge from the cave carrying a crate. A dozen golden objects—from plates and cups to other unidentifiable items—were visible as they jutted out of the top of the wooden crate. The man set the crate down nearby, and when he left, Jacob crept closer and grasped the nearest object he could find and ducked back into the shelter of the bushes and examined it. It was an uncut diamond as big as his fist.

Good God.

Whoever these men were, they had stumbled upon an archaeological find of great importance, and they were looting it dry. The items they were stealing belonged with the descendants of the people who had put them there or, if such people no longer existed, in a museum.

I should leave now, Jacob's inner voice warned him. But the thought of such injustice . . . no. He had to leave. He couldn't put his wife and child at risk. Not for this. He was about to put the diamond back into the crate when he felt it go warm beneath his palm, and a strange humming filled his head. Flashes of light, whispering . . . voices he couldn't quite understand, but he sensed what they wanted.

Keep the diamond. Run now!

He sank back into the foliage, tucked the diamond in a pocket of his cargo pants, and turned to run, only to barrel straight into a man. They both stumbled back. Jacob saw the man loosely clutching a rifle, and he acted fast. He threw a punch that would have made his boxing days at Cambridge look tame. The man hit the ground, out cold, and thankfully not having attracted any attention.

Jacob shook out his fist, stretching his fingers before he leapt over the fallen body and started to run. Once that man woke up, he would tell the others to come after him. Jacob had to get to Amelia and Thorne.

Jacob had gotten a quarter of a mile away when he heard faint shouts behind him. He picked up his pace. Above him, birds were chattering madly and monkeys screamed in warning. It was like the entire jungle was crying out that danger was coming.

He reached the plane and burst inside. "Amelia, grab Thorne! We have to get out of here!"

His wife grabbed their child. Jacob threw the remaining protein bars and water tablets in a bag and slung it over his shoulder. They had made it a hundred yards from the plane when they stumbled right into the path of a silverback gorilla. It thumped its chest with its fists, making a loud *pok—pok—pok* sound as it snarled and charged them.

Jacob shoved his wife behind him and bowed his head.

"Don't look at it. Keep your gaze down," he warned Amelia.

She covered Thorne's head with one hand as they backed up. The male gorilla advanced a few more paces. Jacob's breath came fast as he tried to think and remain calm. The gorilla was pushing them back toward the plane—back toward the gold thieves. He reached a hand behind him, and Amelia laced her fingers in his in silent support.

Suddenly the gorilla's attention lifted above them to something behind them. His lips curled back in a fresh snarl, and he started to charge at whatever he'd seen behind them.

A volley of bullets struck the animal's chest. Blood misted in the air, and the beast collapsed dead at Jacob's feet.

"No!" Despite their current peril, his heart ached for the gorilla's life. With horrifying dread, he and Amelia turned around to face the true danger of the jungle.

"Jacob," Amelia whispered, her hand still in his and her other arm holding their child to her chest.

They faced the group of armed men. A white man, young, possibly twenty or so, seemed to be the one in charge. His pale-blue eyes were so cold that they made Jacob shiver. Jacob knew that he and his family were not going to survive. There was no mercy in those eyes, only cold calculation.

"Please," Jacob said. "Please leave us alone. We won't tell anyone anything." He moved protectively in front of Amelia and his child. He would, without hesitation or thought, give his last breath to protect them.

"How did you get this deep into the forest?" the

young man asked. "The tours don't come this far east."

"Our plane crashed. We were headed for the airfield near the forest guide station." Jacob nodded toward the direction they'd come from.

The man jerked his gun at them. "Show me."

Jacob took Thorne into his arms, and Amelia stuck close to him as they walked back to the crash site. He and his family stood with the Cessna at their backs as the armed men conversed in hushed tones.

"Amelia, we aren't getting out of this alive." He shot her a quick glance before facing the men again.

"Why can't they just let us go?" she asked.

"Because I saw the gold and diamonds they were looting from a cave." He caught her gaze and put a hand lightly, almost casually on the slight bulge of his pocket where he had the diamond.

"Gold?" she echoed. "All of *this* is for gold and diamonds?"

The greed of men ran deep, like the fissures of rocks that exposed the veins of the gold they coveted so badly. And with every ounce of greed, twice the blood would be spilled. Jacob knew better than to bargain with men like these.

The thieves faced them again. The youngest one, the one with the cold eyes, raised his gun at Jacob.

"We've had a little vote. You aren't worth leaving

alive." That was Jacob's only warning before the gun fired.

"Jacob!" Amelia cried out.

The bullet tore through his chest. He reached up slowly and touched the wound as his blood bubbled over his hand. Amelia's voice was distant to his ears now as he fell back against the side of the plane and sank to his knees.

Above him, the exotic birds shrieked a warning that came too late. He choked. The sense of drowning was so frightening, yet he couldn't move, couldn't speak. His vision paled at the edges rather than darkened, as though he was slowly being surrounded by a light, soothing mist. Dimly, he wondered if that was why a person's eyes clouded. It was like death stole over them like an inescapable fog.

It was so hard to think now. He clutched at the last few seconds of his life, and his mind drifted to thoughts of autumn leaves caught upon the wind, carried to places far and away.

⚜

AMELIA SHOVED THORNE BEHIND HER. THE CHILD was stiff and silent with fear. Jacob lay motionless a few feet away. The light in his eyes guttered like a candle in a mighty wind and finally went out. She had no time to grieve—her maternal instincts overrode all else.

"Please, we won't tell anyone. My son's only three. I need to take care of him." Thorne curled one arm around her leg, holding on for his tiny life.

"It's nothing personal. No loose ends."

"Please don't. Not my baby!"

The man almost smiled. "Don't worry, love. I don't kill children."

The man with blue eyes raised his gun again, and Amelia stared him down, defiant to the last as he fired. She collapsed to the ground, Thorne hugging her arm, sniffling as he tried to stay quiet.

"Please don't. Not my baby . . ." She tried with her dying breath to shelter Thorne at her side. It was so hard to breathe. So very hard . . .

"A mother's love—how touching," the man mused thoughtfully as he gazed down at the child. He met Thorne's gaze, and then looked toward Jacob's body. "Search his pockets. I don't want to leave anything someone could use to identify him."

One man searched Jacob's pockets and held up the fat uncut diamond. The man with blue eyes holstered his gun and took the diamond, holding it up with a possessive gleam darkening his eyes.

"Put their bodies inside the plane. I don't want anyone to think they survived the crash, assuming anyone even finds the wreck." He walked away, and the remaining men came toward Jacob.

"What about him?" one of his men asked and nodded at the toddler.

The man with the blue eyes turned back. "He is not to be harmed. Put him in the plane with his parents. I don't kill children, but he'll die out here soon enough. Let nature run its course." Amelia was breathing shallowly now, her limbs cold and numb.

"Don't touch . . . him!" she gasped, choking on her own blood as the men lifted up her beloved husband. "Don't . . ."

Then they came for her. She was already slipping away. Such a funny thing, dying. Once the pain faded, all that was left was quiet silence, like falling asleep on a sunny Saturday afternoon. But it wasn't easy, letting go—not when she left her child behind.

❧

ADROA OKELLO HELD HIS RIFLE LOOSELY, A CANVAS bag of gold slung over one shoulder as he stood inside the crashed plane. Others had carried the bodies in and set them in the chairs. But the boy, the helpless child, wouldn't be parted from his mother. He sat curled on her lap, one hand resting on her lifeless arm, his body trembling as he murmured, asking her to wake up over and over.

Adroa wanted to help the boy. He was no killer, but he'd been paid good money by his boss, the Englishman called Archibald Holt, but who he called Death Eyes in Swahili when he was out of hearing. Adroa had a wife and his own children to feed and he couldn't risk crossing Holt.

The child sniffled, his vivid dark-blue eyes so wide and full of tears that Adroa could not bear it. He was the last of Holt's men inside the plane now. No one would see what he was about to do. He swung the canvas bag off his shoulder and removed one of the gold trinkets they'd stolen from the cave—a gold circlet of leaves like a crown. He held it out to the child. Holt would never know a piece like this had gone missing. And perhaps the gold would distract the child for a little while.

"Be good now," he told the little boy in English and patted the child's silky dark hair. "Stay inside, you hear? Someone will come for you." He didn't want to lie, but what else could he do? Save the boy, and Death Eyes would kill him. Kill the boy, and Death Eyes would kill him.

The boy gazed up at Adroa mutely, his tiny fingers curling around the leafy golden crown. A sudden eerie feeling stole through Adroa. He felt the presence of his ancestors in the shafts of light penetrating the canopy above. Many thousands of years ago, his people had lived in this jungle. They'd built great cities among the trees, and the cave had held their sacred treasure. All of that had been a myth to Adroa until he'd set foot in the cave with Holt and the others a few weeks ago. The glint of gold beneath their pale flashlight beams had almost blinded him. And he'd sensed the anger of the ancient ones in the cave, felt their righteous fury deep within his blood and bones. But they were dead, dead and gone, and had no use for treasure now.

Perhaps it was his imagination, or perhaps it wasn't, but he was sure that he heard a whispered warning among the trees as he left the crashed plane. The whispers murmured that a ghost would rise, crowned in gold, a lord of the jungle returning to avenge his family.

Adroa stumbled back and raced into the jungle to catch up with Holt and the others. He tried to banish the image of that child from his mind, but he knew it would haunt him for the rest of his life.

CHAPTER 2

Half a mile away from where the Haywoods' plane had crashed, a band of gorillas paused at the rush of strange noises in the distance. The rapid sounds were harsh and violent to their ears. Their leader, the silverback Mukisa, had been far ahead of them, scouting the unfamiliar area to ensure their safety. But Mukisa had not returned.

Keza, a young adult female, carried her new infant Akika, one of Mukisa's children, in one arm as she followed the others, trailing Mukisa's scent.

The smell of blood now drifted to them on the wind, and the band grew agitated. Keza held her child tight, ready to run or climb to protect her baby. They continued to track the scent deep into the jungle until they came upon Mukisa's body. He lay face-down, one black palm reaching out in the dirt.

Keza was the only one brave enough to approach her mate's body. She touched his fingers, feeling the coldness, the unnatural stiffness already settling into him. She prodded at his shoulder next, but she knew, as all animals did, that her mate was gone. Their leader was dead.

Sunya, one of Mukisa's younger sons, came forward and grunted softly, declaring himself the new dominant male. He faced no opposition. He led them forward, in the direction Mukisa had been taking to reach the river, where they could find water.

Strange new smells filled Keza's senses—an animal she did not recognize, along with an acrid burning scent that left her jittery and anxious for the safety of her infant, Akika. They soon entered a clearing where a great white shape lay in the underbrush.

A sharp cry came from within the white mass. Most of the gorillas stepped back, pressing their knuckles hard against the ground, ready for an attack. The cry came again, and something deep in Keza's breast tightened. This was the cry of a child. A cry for help. Her mothering instincts were strong with her first child, and she would respond to any call in need. She approached the white shape alone, still cradling her sweet Akika to her chest. When the cry came again, Keza pushed her way carefully into the dark hole.

Her eyes adjusted to the dim light, and she halted

as her nose picked up the scent of death again, and that strange animal smell she didn't recognize. She moved closer. It was a sound of distress, not unlike her own babe's feeble cries.

A white-faced creature was looking at her, its eyes blue like the sky. Keza tilted her head, puzzled. She had never seen a creature like this. It had no hair covering its body, just some on the top of its head. The babe held out something that glinted in the dying light, but that object held no interest to Keza. She hooted softly at the baby creature and reached a finger toward it.

The child dropped the shiny object and curled tiny fingers around her thick black digit. In that instant, Keza bonded with the strange child. She reached for him, curving her other arm around his small body, and nestled him beside her little Akika. The child shifted, sniffled, and then grew quiet. She could hear his belly growl with hunger.

Sunya might not wish for this infant to stay in their band since he was not Sunya's child, but she was older than Sunya and fierce with a mother's love. She would kill him if he tried to harm either of her sons. Even across species, a mother and child could love without question. There were many harsh rules that governed Keza's world, but one ruled above all, and that was a mother's love.

THORNE CLUNG TO THE MOTHER GORILLA, HIS belly growling. He didn't understand why Mummy and Daddy did not wake up, no matter how much he asked them to or cried. But the black beast from his favorite book had answered his cries.

G. Gorilla.

The gorilla had crept toward him, and he'd stopped crying. He nuzzled his face against her dark bristly hair and gazed wide-eyed at the baby gorilla next to him. The baby's reddish-brown eyes were wide as he gazed back at Thorne.

As Thorne was carried into the jungle, his ears took in the rustle of leaves and the buzz of insects, the exotic sound of birds and monkeys. The blend of sounds turned into a gentle symphony that lulled him to sleep between the warmth of Keza's chest and the humid jungle air.

The band of gorillas stopped after several hours and settled in a safe, dense spot to feed and rest. Mist rolled in around them, thick and cooling to the skin. Thorne was kept within reach of Keza, who set Akika down beside him.

The little human boy watched the gorilla who had carried him to safety, her black and silver fur blending to a burnished bronze at the top of her head. In that moment she was beautiful to him, more beautiful than anything he'd ever seen before.

She was his mother now; he understood a mother's caring touch as she brushed her fingers over his head, and his tiny heart filled with infinite love for her.

❧

KEZA PUZZLED OVER HER NEW CHILD'S TINY fingers, similar yet not quite the same as Akika's. She ruffled a hand over the dark hair on his head. It was soft, far softer than her own. She plucked gently at his ears, checking for mites. He made a gurgling noise, baring his teeth, but it didn't seem threatening to her.

She curled her lips back, showing her own sharp white teeth, and he clapped his tiny hands together. The little smacking sound was odd. Keza wondered if he was trying to show his strength at so young an age. She curled her fist and gave a powerful smack to her chest. The noise startled the child, and he grew still. But after a moment, he curled his own fist and slapped it against himself in imitation. Keza hooted in approval. He learned quickly. That was good. The jungle held many dangers, and the quicker this hairless ape could learn, the safer he would be.

The other gorillas in the band warily watched the

young child. Sunya snorted and bared his teeth, but one quelling look from Keza and he came no closer toward them.

"I'm Thorne." The child spoke with a strange tongue. She grunted at him.

He tapped his chest. "Thorne." Then he climbed up her legs and perched on her lap and tapped her chest, gazing deeply into her eyes as though waiting for her to respond. She seemed to understand that he wished to know her name.

"Keza." She spoke in her own language, and he repeated the sound. Then he gently placed a hand on Akika's tiny arm, his questioning eyes so full of yearning that Keza became spellbound by him.

"Akika . . . brother . . . friend." She spoke to him in her tongue, and he replied, imitating her. Though their sounds were merely a pleasant noise to Thorne at first, the thoughts behind those noises grew ever clearer. In time he would learn their language more clearly than the one he had been born into.

He was quick to learn a dozen words that first day. She taught him which plants to eat, like stems, bamboo shoots, and fruits. He favored fruits the most, and she let him eat those. At first he was not strong enough to hold on to her back like Akika, but after a few weeks he could curl an arm around her neck and hold on just as well as her other son.

As the days passed, Keza settled into her life as a

mother to her two children. The band of twelve gorillas she lived with were always tolerant, and often indulgent to both Akika and Thorne.

It soon became clear that Thorne had deft control of his hands and could peel bark on trees and could climb with the ease of the younger apes. He was slow to grow and did not prefer to walk on his knuckles, but Keza let him do as he wished. She saw in her own way as he grew stronger that his balance was better when he was upright. Every now and then Keza would walk upright with him, holding Thorne's tiny hand in her right and Akika's hand in her left.

Joy filled her whenever she saw her children playing together, wrestling and growling. She hooted and huffed in encouragement. Akika, the child of her body, and Thorne, the child of her heart. She could not be happier.

When Akika was nearly a year old, he fell climbing and a nasty set of spines from a bush below were embedded in his arm. Keza could not pull them free. But Thorne, with his slender fingers, stroked his knuckles over Akika's face and head in a gentle, soothing motion before he began to ease the spines from the distressed gorilla.

Akika watched his pale-skinned brother with soft, loving eyes, and Thorne bared his teeth in the way that Keza now understood was not a threat, but his way of showing joy. Keza knew she had made a good decision taking the hairless ape into her arms that day, and her love for him became infinite.

⁂

THIRTEEN YEARS LATER

Thorne stood at the edge of the still pool that fed into a small waterfall below. His family drank handfuls of water hesitantly at the edge. Gorillas could not swim easily and kept well away from it for fear of drowning, or the other dangers that might lurk within it. But Thorne did not fear the water. He was drawn to it, fixated by the way the canopy of moss-covered trees reflected perfectly in its glassy surface.

He crept up to the shore of the pool and peered into the water, glimpsing his face reflected back at him. This was not the first time he had looked into the water, but it was the first time he truly noticed how different he looked compared to his family.

Thorne's face was narrow, with a thinner mouth, and his eyes were the color of an evening sky. A scruffy layer of dark-brown hair grew around his jaw and his loins but not over the rest of his body. His limbs were sleek, his muscles defined and yet so different in so many ways from his brother.

Thorne studied the different shape of his fingers compared to Akika's. Even his feet were different. He'd never been able to grasp things with his toes as gracefully as his brother could. He'd been too afraid and ashamed to compare his body to the others. He knew what they called him in their grunts and huffs. *The deformed hairless ape.*

Perhaps he was not deformed after all. Perhaps he was formed as he should be, and he simply was not an ape? The idea, once formed within him, gave him a greater curiosity, a need for answers. Some nights when he lay alone, a little way from the other gorillas as they slept, he let his mind wander, and strange dreams came in that moment just between sleep and waking. Dreams of apes who looked like him, their voices soft, full of love . . . and other strange dreams of a world that in this lush jungle land seemed impossible.

Perhaps they were dreams born of fevered nights when the humidity threatened to choke him and he sought refuge high in the treetops, thrusting his head above the canopy to feel the wind on his face.

One truth that always came back to him, no matter how much it hurt him to think about it, was that he had not always been a gorilla. Once, long ago, he had been something, *someone* else.

Thorne touched the surface of the water, creating ripples that distorted his image in the pool. A quivering took hold of him as for the first time in his young life he accepted that he was truly *not* like his family.

G. Gorilla . . . A soft voice spoke to him through the mists of time. The forest around him almost seemed to hum in response.

He knew that he was something else. But what? Thorne's heart grew heavy with shame at not being Akika's true brother, but there was a glimmer of curiosity that defined his species—though he did not yet know he belonged to that species.

Thorne stared at the surface of the water.

If he was not a gorilla, then perhaps he could swim the way he'd seen the leopards do when they crossed rivers and lakes. They moved slowly, sleekly through the water, pawing their front legs in forward circular motions and kicking with their back legs. Thorne was not as big or as heavy as his kin, so perhaps he could do the same? He'd noticed he had a different mobility in his body, so it was entirely possible that he was capable of swimming. There was only one way to find out.

He flung himself recklessly into the pool. Keza's scream of terror was muted as Thorne sank beneath the surface. He opened his eyes, seeing the murky depths of the watery world around him. His bare feet touched the bottom of the pool. He coiled himself tight and pushed up until he surged into the light and gasped sweet air. He moved his arms, testing their effectiveness, and soon he was pulling himself toward the shore, where his mother was pacing and wailing in panic.

Thorne, a little weary after such a new activity, crawled out of the water, breathing deeply. Keza rushed to him, balled a fist, and thumped his side with one hand, her touch gentle even as she reprimanded his behavior. Then she grasped his head and pulled him around, looking him over for injury.

He hooted in reassurance at his mother and grasped her large solid hands with his own, holding them to his skin. Gorillas thrived on physical touch, they lived for contact with one another, and Thorne was no different. He craved his mother's brushing caresses over his hair and the light thumps of her loosely balled fist against his chest in greeting.

He glanced back once more at the pool, and a deep longing for more answers and more truths filled him. But he would have to return when his mother was not there to fuss over him.

The band finished drinking and worked their way into a group of fruit trees to eat their evening meal and rest. Thorne climbed the nearest mango tree; he alone among his family was still the most comfortable at such an activity. Once gorillas aged, they stayed closer to the ground.

Thorne plucked some ripe-smelling fruit from a tree and tossed them down to the gorillas below, where they divided the food. But he did not join them. He clutched a pair of mangoes in his hand and climbed higher in a hagenia tree until he leaned against the thin branches that formed the canopy. He pushed his head through the spreading branches and looked out over the tops of the forest that stretched for hundreds of miles around. Above him the sky was inky black, with a vibrant spread of glittering stars.

Stars . . . He knew what they were. Well, not exactly, but he knew the word. *Stars*. The word felt different on his tongue. It was not from the language of the birds, the leopards, or the gorillas. It was a language that was softer, clearer, yet just as beautiful as the languages he spoke now with love in his heart. The word *stars* remained inside him like a well-kept secret, spreading a warmth he could not explain as he ate his fruit and gazed upon the expanse far above him. There were feelings, not quite memories, that churned within him, calling in soft whispers.

Remember who you are. Remember . . .

❧

THOUSANDS OF MILES AWAY

Cameron Haywood stood at the window of his study in Somerset Hall, the ancestral home of the earldom of Somerset in England. He held a glass of scotch and gazed upon the same stars, though muted somewhat by the distant city lights.

Thirteen years. Had it really been that long since his older brother, Jacob, had been lost in the Ugandan forest with his wife and child? It felt like a lifetime ago. He had never wanted to become the Earl of Somerset. He would give *everything* to have his family back.

Thirteen years ago, he had done all that he could to find his brother. He had sent search parties, tried to locate the plane, and bribed every official for any information. He'd flown there a dozen times, scouring the impenetrable forest, even calling the names of his loved ones until he lost his voice.

Cameron went to his desk, turning his back to the stars. The sounds of a party going on in his house downstairs gave him no joy at the prospect of mingling among the powerful men and women of England. Today would have been his nephew's sixteenth birthday.

"Cameron." His wife, Isabelle, stuck her head into his office. "Our guests are waiting. Duty calls, I'm afraid. Lofty is entertaining everyone with tales, but you know he can't do that forever. Well, he can, actually, but we shouldn't let him." Isabelle almost smiled. Jordie Lofthouse had been the only one who could make Cameron or Isabelle smile in all these years.

"I'm coming, darling," he sighed. He touched the faces of Jacob, Amelia, and little Thorne in a framed photo on his desk before he went out to meet his wife.

"You look pale," Isabelle murmured in concern. She looked up at him with those lovely gray eyes of hers, eyes that had bewitched him long before Jacob's death. Isabelle had married him before he knew his life would change forever. She hadn't wanted their sudden change in circumstances any more than he had. They'd both wanted to be free, to live a life without the constraints of the titles that had been thrust upon them.

"It's Thorne's birthday today. He would have been sixteen." Cameron rubbed his eyes with his thumb and forefinger. Isabelle brushed his dark hair back from his face with her fingers.

"I know. I remembered this morning. Why don't I send everyone away and we can have a quiet night together by the fire?"

He almost chuckled. "Banish the peers of the realm from the halls of Somerset? As tempting as it sounds, I don't think that's a good idea." He pressed a kiss to her temple. "I shall just put on a brave face and get on with the night. It won't be the first time."

Cameron and his wife descended the grand staircase into the waiting crowd below with diplomatic smiles. But his heart, at least part of it, still searched for answers in the dark heart of the jungle in Africa.

FOUR YEARS LATER

Thorne heard the creatures long before he saw them. Three animals stumbling through the underbrush of the forest. Their disregard for leaving evidence of their passage left an easy trail to follow. The sounds they made, a unique mix of complex utterances, were musical, like birdsong rather than the deep vocal chorus-like language of the gorillas.

Curious, he crept along the massive stretching branches of the trees above these creatures as he sought a clearer look. They continued to vocalize in their nonsense language as they stopped and sat down at the base of the trees.

He slid lower, using thick vines to support his body as he tried to see their faces. They wore strange animal skins, very different from the kob deer pelt that covered Thorne's vulnerable parts.

His gorilla family wore no such skins. Their bodies were more compact, and their posture lent them far more natural protection. Thorne felt exposed and vulnerable, so after killing his first deer, he began to wear animal skins as a way to protect himself. He wasn't quite sure how he'd come by the idea—except perhaps to say he'd dreamed it. Visions of animals like him wearing gleaming pieces of something on their necks and arms. They'd showed him in wild, quick flashes in these dreams how to hunt deer, how to use the shale rocks to skin them. He'd been ashamed to hunt in front of the gorillas, who did not eat deer, so he had gone much deeper into the forest to hunt.

He'd refined his technique now to have a dried bit of leather from the deer with which to fashion himself a way to tie the pelt tight around his waist without worry of it falling off while he swung from vines and climbed.

The creatures he stalked now were almost fully covered in such skins.

One of the creatures removed a covering from his head, and Thorne's mouth parted in shock. These animals were like him, yet not. Their skin was dark, like the rich bark of a mahogany tree and just like the creatures in his dreams who'd taught him how to survive. Their hands and limbs were not formed like the gorillas'. They were exactly like Thorne's. For the first time in seventeen years, he was staring at a face like his own.

"Gorilla."

The word was the only one that he recognized in the stream of sounds pouring from their lips as they spoke to one another.

A sudden, painful flash of memory, an image of a gorilla upon wood. No, not wood—*paper*.

A face like his gazed down at him, a female with a

bright smile and golden hair . . . smiles . . . How had he forgotten what a smile was?

His lips curved into a grin, and he huffed excitedly until he saw one of the creatures lift a long brown stick, pointing it at a small monkey perched on a tree branch not far from Thorne.

The creature held the stick close to his face, and there was a violent *bang!* Thorne was so startled that he lost his grip on the vines and plummeted to the forest floor. He landed catlike on the ground, not ten feet from the creatures. One of them screamed and pointed at him. The male who held the loud stick turned it on Thorne, hollering. There was another deafening *bang!*

Pain knifed through Thorne's arm, and he howled with rage as he stood to his full height. He curled his fists and beat savagely on his chest, bearing his teeth as he'd seen Sunya do a thousand times before. The creatures shouted back, but fear widened their eyes and they scrambled away. In their haste to flee, one tripped, his head hitting the base of a knotted tree as the others left him behind.

Thorne stopped a short distance from the body and crouched, studying him. The creature had different feet than him, and his face held no hair along his jaw and mouth like Thorne. He reached out, his fingers touching the male's face. His skin appeared smooth, but beneath his fingertips, Thorne felt the bristle of hair, much like his had felt when he'd been younger. Despite his size, perhaps he was not yet grown?

Suddenly the male's eyes snapped open, and he stared in horror at Thorne.

"Gorilla." Thorne repeated the word, finding it easier to say than he expected. He tapped his own chest and repeated. "Gorilla."

"What?" the man said. "No. Not gorilla."

Not. That word Thorne recognized too.

The male looked him over, as amazed by Thorne as Thorne was by him. Eventually he nodded and tapped his chest.

"Human," the male said. "Man."

Thorne stared at him, bewildered as the tongue that he had been born to speak came back to him in hazy flashes.

"Boy," he said.

B is for boy. You're a boy, Thorne. A female's face flashed in his mind, the woman he'd glimpsed in his mind with sunlight-gold hair who smiled.

"G is for gorilla." Thorne whispered the words, his voice rasping. He had not used his vocal cords like this in years. It almost hurt to speak.

"You speak English?"

"Ing-leesh?" Thorne murmured the familiar word.

"Yes, English," the male said with excitement, smiling.

"Yes," Thorne echoed. He pressed his calloused palm on the man's chest, their eyes locked on each other. Around them the jungle murmured softly, and Thorne smiled as he looked at the man.

"Friend?" Thorne asked. There was something about the man's face, a kindness and quick intelligence in his eyes that made Thorne trust him.

The man nodded, now solemn. "Friend."

WANT TO KNOW WHAT HAPPENS NEXT? GET THE book HERE!

EMMA CASTLE

Dark and Edgy Romance

OTHER TITLES BY EMMA CASTLE

Standalones

Love in the Wild- A Tarzan Retelling

Devastate Me

The Lord and the Labyrinth (coming 2021)

Unlikely Heroes

*can be read as standalones

Midnight with the Devil - Book 1

A Wilderness Within - Book 2

Sci-Fi Romance - The Krinar World

The Krinar Eclipse by Lauren Smith - Book 1

The Krinar Code by Emma Castle - Book 2

ABOUT THE AUTHOR

Emma Castle has always loved reading but didn't know she loved romance until she was enduring the trials of law school. She discovered the dark and sexy world of romance novels and since then has never looked back! She loves writing about sexy, alpha male heroes who know just how to seduce women even if they are a bit naughty about it. When Emma's not writing, she may be obsessing over her favorite show Supernatural where she's a total Team Dean Winchester kind of girl!

If you wish to be added to Emma's new release newsletter feel free to contact Emma using the Sign up link on her website at www.emmacastlebooks.com or email her at emma@emmacastlebooks.com!